Goodbye, Evil Eye

Gloria DeVidas Kirchheimer

Goodbye, Evil Eye

STORIES

HM
HOLMES & MEIER
New York / London

Published in the United States of America 2000 by
Holmes & Meier Publishers, Inc.
160 Broadway New York, NY 10038

Designed by Jackie Schuman

This book has been printed on acid-free paper.

Some of the stories in this collection have appeared elsewhere in slight-
ly different form: "Food of Love" in *Shmate*, in *The Tribe of Dina*, and
in *Follow My Footprints: Changing Images of Women in American Jewish
Fiction*; "A Case of Dementia" in *North American Review* and *Shaking
Eve's Tree*; "Arbitration" in *Kansas Quarterly* and *Sephardic-American
Voices: Two Hundred Years of a Literary Legacy*; "The Voyager" in
Kansas Quarterly and *Sephardic-American Voices*; "A Skirmish in the
Desert" in *Bridges*; "Traffic Manager" in *Cimarron Review*. A different
version of "Goodbye, Evil Eye" appeared in *NASA WI News* under the
title "A Story of Blood." The preface appeared in *Jewish Currents* as
"Talking in Tongues."

Library of Congress Cataloging-in-Publication Data

Kirchheimer, Gloria DeVidas.
    Goodbye, evil eye: stories / Gloria DeVidas Kirchheimer.
        p. cm.
    ISBN 0-8419-1404-4 (cloth : alk. paper)
    1. Sephardim—New York (State)—New York—Anecdotes. 2.
Jews—New York
    (State)—New York Anecdotes. 3. Kirchheimer, Gloria DeVidas—
Family—Anecdotes. I.
    Title.

F128.9.J5 K56 2000
974.7'1004924—dc21
00-020443

974.7/
K632g

Manufactured in the United States of America

For Manny

For Manny

The author wishes to express her appreciation to
Yaddo and the MacDowell Colony,
and to the New York Foundation for the Arts for
its sponsorship of this project.

CONTENTS

CONTENTS

PREFACE

In our house, the direct statement was seldom used as a vehicle for communication. Innuendo was the order of the day, whether the language was Ladino, French, or English: for instance, a suggestion that I remove my sweater meant that my mother was feeling warm and wanted me to open the window. If I was told that my uncle considered me his favorite niece, I knew I was being reproached for not having sent him a birthday card. Like the baclava my mother made, our language was swathed in layers designed to sweeten reality.

A child growing up in that household needed to be in a constant state of alertness since things were seldom what they seemed. Occasionally I was caught off guard, American kid that I was, accustomed to the plain talk that surrounded me at school. "If you should happen to pass the grocery store . . . " my mother would say.

I was often exasperated by her coyness. Why didn't she just come out and say what she meant?

Perhaps this was a way of shielding against an outright rejection. After all, I might have balked or possibly refused to do what she asked. Later I came to realize that millions of people throughout the Middle East practiced this mode of communication, which drove Americans crazy. In any case, no-risk language was the rule among our people, with some exceptions—like my father cursing his boss (but not to his face) or the salty language used by one of our neighbors, Hermana Bohor, an elderly widow from my father's hometown of Izmir, Turkey.

When I was about five or six, Hermana Bohor gave a party in honor of her youngest son who had volunteered for the Lincoln Brigade and was going off to Spain. He would thus be the only Sephardic person we knew of to return to our ancestral homeland from which we Jews had been expelled in 1492, a memory so vivid to all of us it might have happened yesterday. To hear the enthusiasm expressed by the adults, the recommendations of what sights to see, you would have thought he was going as a tourist instead of to a bloody war.

I was semihysterical with excitement because of the singing and dancing in that small apartment. My mother was playing the mandolin, someone else had a tambourine; even Hermana Bohor in her long brown dress was up and gyrating in a stately belly dance. The other children and I were fighting over the privilege of cranking up the Victrola so we could hear for the tenth time a comic record of a patient in a dentist's chair crying out in agony, "*Me duele! Me duele!*" It hurts! It hurts! His cries worked us into a frenzy and we dashed back and forth shrieking at the adults.

One of the boys dared me to run up to Hermana Bohor and scream an obscenity at her, the Ladino (and Spanish) word for backside. As far as I had observed, only men who worked in the import–export business could say it with impunity, although I had once overheard our hostess utter it with no ill effect. With fear in my soul I went to her and whispered the word in her ear. She reared back and wagged a friendly finger at me. "One doesn't say this out loud, my little one."

"But," I protested, "how come you can say it?"

She folded her hands across her stomach and said smugly, "*Yo se madre*"—I am a mother. No other explanation was needed. At that moment, beyond the privilege of wearing lipstick or the right to stay up late, the prospect of an enhanced vocabulary made me long for motherhood.

I walked sedately back to my companions as though already in training for my future role as a parent. My own parents, however, were cavorting with abandon like the rest of the adults. One of my uncles was shouting endearments in Turkish to a red-headed woman I had never seen before. The guest of honor, the young man who was going off to fight the fascists, was stuffing coins into a neighbor's décolletage.

Years later I wondered why everyone had been so gay and lively at this party, in view of the fact that the young man was about to risk his life. For the longest time after the party I wanted to ask my parents if he was going to die. But I had never heard the word "death" actually articulated in any language in my home.

Even my favorite goldfish, which was found floating on its side one evening, was said to have rejoined its ancestors. I found this a ludicrous description and began to realize that my parents and I truly did not speak the same language.

While avoidance of the direct statement was ingrained, so too was unequivocal possession of Spanish, our ancestral tongue, and of French as well, the language my parents had learned at the schools established by the Alliance Française Israélite throughout the Ottoman Empire.

Their proprietorship of these two languages manifested itself in entirely different ways. Spanish was ours by hereditary right. We had lived in Spain for generations and had taken the language with us in our travels, where it had evolved into the form we knew—Ladino. To my mother, encountering Puerto Ricans, Dominicans, and Cubans in the streets and stores of our Washington Heights neighborhood in Manhattan, their Spanish was a travesty of the one true tongue. No matter that some of our Spanish words had not been spoken since the fifteenth century or that some of our words were not Spanish but rather Turkish or Arabic or Hebrew. We were still the grandees. Should someone play a flamenco song on the radio, we were up and stamping our feet and clicking our fingers. The rhythm and lyrics were in our blood, make no mistake about it. Little did they know, those Hispanic waiters and saleswomen who tried to insult us. What a tongue lashing they would receive, to my great embarrassment. "We are Spanish," my mother told these errant proletarians. (We were also Arabic or French or Turkish, depending on the venue, since my mother considered fluency the only requisite for nationality.)

But French—ah, the language of the gods, of refinement and poetry. At the Alliance schools my parents not only learned to conjugate but also memorized the classics: the sonorous verses of Lamartine, Victor Hugo, Alfred de Vigny, verses recited at the drop of a hat while standing in line at a bus stop or at the supermarket. My father was also fond of barking out commands or proverbs in French: "*Avis aux amateurs*"—Watch your step. Or "*Pierre qui roule n'amasse pas mousse*"—The rolling stone gathers no moss. (To this day I'm still unsure about whether or not it is advantageous to gather the moss.)

We were aristocrats because we knew French, we could tussle with any maître d', we didn't have to read the subtitles at the movies, and we caught the nuances of *Carmen*, our ideal opera since it was set in Seville and sung in French.

World War II brought a flood of German Jewish refugees to our neighborhood. Although filled with compassion for their suffering, my parents were hard put to listen to them speaking German without wincing. Almost as grating were the newcomers' attempts to speak English in public to avoid identification with their hated compatriots. Not that my parents spoke without accents. Still, my mother could claim that she had learned English while her native Egypt was still under British dominion.

One mitigating factor in favor of the new arrivals was their attitude toward us, the Sephardim. Although they openly patronized Eastern Jews, they willingly deferred to us as being the crème de la crème. And unlike some of our neighbors, they understood that one did not have to know Yiddish to be Jewish.

I later became engaged to marry a German Jewish refugee, and even though this would be a kind of inter-marriage, my parents did not consider that I was marrying too far beneath me. My husband-to-be took a perverse delight in introducing me to his fellow refugees as his Spanish fiancée. This did not prevent them from speaking to me in German. When I said that I didn't know the language, they expressed surprise and advised me to learn it.

My parents worried about the linguistic heritage I would bequeath to their future grandchildren: a smattering of Ladino, some French poems, and God knew what Wagnerian excesses. As it turned out, the children grew up on the streets of New York and pride of language came to revolve around English and all its permutations. Still, echoes of ancestral tongues continue to fill my dreams.

Gloria DeVidas Kirchheimer

One who is burned by the soup will blow on the yogurt.

—*Old Ladino proverb*

Goodbye, Evil Eye

Food of Love

A woman drags a shopping cart up the 181st Street hill, looking furtively over her shoulder. She is sixty-five, wears a kerchief, and the hem of her coat is undone in·the back. Another woman appears with a cart. After a hurried conversation a parcel is transferred from the first cart to the second.

This is not a dope drop. The first woman is my mother who, after evading my father's questions with the excuse that she is going shopping, has secretly entrusted ten pounds of phyllo dough to her friend who will store it sub rosa in her refrigerator. My retired father does not like Mother to engage in extramarital culinary activities. With the same subterfuge she might employ to meet a lover, she sneaks out to bake delicacies for the organization of which she is president. Because she has interests outside the home, my father calls her a part-time wife. "Why don't you throw me out like a dog?"

he says whenever she pleads an important committee meeting.

A tigress to her board members, my mother is too timid to go to a box office and buy theater tickets; though she has arranged gala functions for hundreds of people at the best hotels, she cannot bring herself to enter a public library for fear that she will not know how to ask for a library card.

However, within the confines of the synagogue where her organization has its office, she is—as Isabella was queen of all the Americas—queen of all Sephardic womanhood.

She is forced to work with a vice president who lacks authenticity. A descendant of Revolutionary War generals, the woman is made to feel like an outcast. She was elected because her last name is embroidered on seat cushions and inscribed on the Declaration of Independence. Mother gives her useful work to do, stuffing envelopes. What can she know of Sephardic culture, a woman who cooks with safflower oil?

The event for which Mother is preparing is a fundraising luncheon in her honor, to be held in the synagogue community room. The entertainment will consist of a Sephardic sing-along and a short lecture with slides on Our Unique Heritage, designed to wring some money out of our brethren, particularly the Sephardim from Salonika, many of whom are regarded as moguls of the garment business. Their wives cook with olive oil and have been discouraged from aiding in the kitchen by the faction from Izmir.

This is an orthodox synagogue, though half the members travel on the Sabbath to attend services. Mother cooks with a grain of salt and, in her fantasy, with a little unconsecrated cheese which she sprinkles onto the spinach pastries when no one is looking. Hawkeyed, the rabbi's wife watches to see that all is kosher. She comes from Rhodes where (Mother says) they speak an inferior Ladino, the now archaic Spanish we carried with us after the Expulsion.

Long before the luncheon takes place I know I will be approached to attend. Daughters usually attend their mothers' functions, however dull. For years I was successful in avoiding them, but this time it will be difficult. It is Mother's show and she will receive a plaque.

Knowing she will never ask me outright, I wait. Campaigning starts early.

Invited for lunch at my apartment one Saturday, two months before the event, she arrives bearing her usual food parcel. She has never come to my house and eaten my food. Perhaps some bread and coffee, but otherwise she is her own caterer. She wants to spare me the trouble.

"Umm, isn't this good," she says, licking powdered sugar from her fingers. It could be sawdust for the effort it takes me to swallow.

She has brought a new dress to show me. Do I think it suitable for the luncheon?

"What luncheon?" I ask.

The luncheon. She expects two hundred people.

There is already a waiting list. They have hired Aryeh the accordionist and his international band. Did I know they made a recording recently?

"A lot of people make recordings."

"You and I could make one. You have such a lovely voice. I know so many songs. Soon our music will die out if young people like you don't preserve it."

To parricide and fratricide we now add culturicide, with I myself the first offender.

I crumple up her foil wrappings and stuff them into the overfull trash can.

"Relax," Mother says. "I'll clean up, you rest." This is a woman who always insists on carrying the fifty-pound grocery load on the grounds that I look tired.

Now she is hovering over my electric typewriter. "Does it give you shocks?" she asks, standing back a respectful foot and a half.

"Sometimes." All those xxxx'd-out lines.

Watching her reach out to touch the keys, I can't help remembering the time I demonstrated to her the instant cash machines found at most banks.

We were short of money one day while shopping on Fifth Avenue. I found a bank, and she watched me set the process in motion. When the computer screen said, *Hello, is there anything I can do?* she shrieked with wonder. When it asked if I wished to proceed in English or Spanish, she clutched her throat and said, "*Que maravilla!*" Reading over my shoulder, she said that the computer was more polite than the bank tellers she dealt with. I invited her to take the money from the open cylinder but to be quick about it or risk having her hand clamped in its turning maw.

"Do you know," she said when the transaction was completed, "an ignorant person might think there was a devil in there. I mean someone who is superstitious." Then she uttered an imprecation in Arabic to the effect that the evil eye should keep its distance from us and our loved ones.

Her campaign to get me to the luncheon is spread over several weeks. One day she asks, "Did I tell you that Professor Asher Halifa will be addressing us?" I had once made the error of saying that I had read an article of his in *Commentary*.

Another time: "You have a beautiful print dress. You don't wear it enough." Translation: "Wear it to the luncheon." I say nothing. And finally: "I have a ticket reserved for you. It's a nice table, all young people."

I consult my calendar, playing for time. The date is filled. "But Mother, I'm seeing a matinée that Sunday."

"Do you have to go?"

"I don't *have* to go, I *want*—"

"No problem then. They'll exchange the ticket. You have plenty of time."

Trying to salvage some pride, I offer to pay my way to the luncheon but she won't allow it. It's for a good cause. "Relax," she says. It is her battle cry.

The day before the luncheon she calls me. Do I have a tape recorder?

"I have an old machine. The sound is not very good."

"You know we have Aryeh and his accordion. If you feel like taping the music . . ."

"Mother," I say, "I will not *feel* like taping. If you want me to, just say so and I'll be glad to do it. I'll go and buy some tape."

"No, why should you, all that bother. It's too complicated."

"It's not complicated. If you want it, I'll do it. Really, Mom."

"No, no. Forget about it. It's all right."

It's not all right. I should have volunteered immediately of course. Another black mark against this unnatural daughter.

At the luncheon I am embraced by people who knew me when I was a little girl, handsome men and beautiful women with names like Diamante, Joya, Fortunée. "Will you sing for us? You have such a lovely voice." As a teenager I sang here a few times, accompanying myself with primitive guitar chords. I sang with my American accent songs that brought tears to their eyes. It was a phase, folksinging. I haven't been in this building for years.

Mother makes a welcoming speech thanking her vice president and conveying regrets from the distinguished professor Asher Halifa who was to have addressed us today. The main drawing card as far as I was concerned. No wonder she was afraid to tell me.

Mother's speech is concise and charming. She worries

needlessly about her English. My father is watching her as though he has just fallen in love with her. They met forty years ago after a fortune-teller predicted that a dark stranger from Turkey would carry her off from Alexandria. She was twenty-three then, teaching French in an Arabic school, working to support her family while her brothers were at the university. Her father, a dapper gentleman who wore spats and a boutonnière, was a gambler. My grandmother had learned to read, rare for a woman in those days in that country. Even now, my mother talks wistfully about taking college courses but is afraid people will laugh at her. She has always been interested in literature and can recite entire scenes from Racine and Corneille. She used to do it often—at home, in buses, and especially in front of my friends. If she weren't worried about my father catching her, she would watch the advanced Italian course given at seven in the morning on television.

The rabbi makes a speech. In spite of his degrees and erudition, his public relations manner, and his Sephardic wife, he is barely tolerated as a man of the somewhat worn cloth. An Ashkenazi presiding over a Sephardic congregation, he doesn't need to tell us how unique we are as he invites us to go from strength to strength.

Mother is everywhere as people begin to eat. I invite her to sit but she says she doesn't have to eat. Aryeh is playing tunes from a popular Yiddish-American musical on his accordion, and Mother is incensed. She whispers something to him and he switches in mid-chord to a Greek song. Five women, all in their sixties, walk up to the stage and begin to dance. There is a soupçon of belly dance movement but not enough to cause embarrassment. Though the Greek song is about a whore, the rabbi is beaming. One of the women puts a coin on her forehead and throws her head back, arching her whole body. The others make a circle around her. The rest of the audience is clapping in time. A man leaps onto the stage—he must be at least seventy-two—and whips out a handkerchief. The woman with the coin takes hold of a corner of the handkerchief, the man gets down on one knee, and the music speeds up. At the last chord, Mother takes the microphone and announces that dessert is being served.

Now it is time for the plaque. The vice president, in perfect Vassar English, thanks the lady who has given so much of herself. Mother is blowing her nose. I notice a run in her stocking; one shoe has been slipped off. I know she would like nothing better than to loosen her girdle.

The ovation forces Mother back up to the mike. No more speeches, she promises, and suggests we get on with the sing-along. She wants only to say how happy she is that her daughter could be here today to honor her, and they all know how much joy her daughter used to give them with her beautiful voice but "She said, 'Mother, please don't ask me to sing,' and so I won't ask her—"

Pandemonium—my name shouted from every corner of the room, spoons tinkling against the demitasses. The accordion starts whooping like a rusty car engine. Mother smiles, shrugs—it is out of her hands.

People push me out of my seat and up to the stage. "Only if you sing with me," I say, trying not to cry out. They have song sheets but they don't need them. The accordion helps, Mother helps, I sing. I'll get them, I'll get her, they'll be eating out of the palm of my hand. People put down their cups, their baklava, leaning back and sighing. They sing with me in Ladino, songs about their countries, the almond trees, the sea that brings no letters, the daughters in exile, the smoldering mountains. Why have I waited so long to do this? Looking at her, my mother, I understand for the first time what it is to have a "maternal language." I feel that I am singing in tongues, astonishing myself with those archaic syllables, these Moorish melodies. I could swear I smell jasmine blossoms.

"Isn't she grand?" Mother says to the audience, at last. While she is making her financial report, I escape to the ladies room and wash my hands with the kosher soap.

I return to hear Aryeh play a flourish and the start of a lively Arabic song. The curtain that was drawn across the stage now parts, revealing my mother transformed into a houri, a harem woman clad in gold-embroidered silk pantaloons, a silk blouse and vest, pointed velvet slippers with coins jingling at their tips, a silk kerchief over her hair with a fringe of coins on her forehead, finger cymbals in her hands. I stand up. I have never seen this outfit. Where does she keep it? Why did she never show it to me? It must be at least a hundred and fifty years old. It belongs in the Metropolitan Museum or on me. She shakes her shoulders and starts to sing in Arabic, and the people go mad with delight. She leans into the microphone, still shaking her shoulders in rhythm. "Sing, everyone. You like it?" Roars, whistles, pounding on the tables. "It's to make up for my lack of voice. We want to give you your money's worth."

A woman with a face like a gnarled pomegranate stretches out her hands to my mother, then makes her way to me and kisses me on both cheeks as though to confer upon me the Légion d'Honneur, which I deserve today.

"The truth," Mother says on the phone later that night. "From you I want the truth."

"Really, you were great."

"Honest?" She giggles.

"Would I lie?"

"Not you. You always speak your mind. You are direct, like me."

I shuffle the papers on my desk while she talks. I had just been contemplating writing her an irate and formal note about her treachery to me at the microphone. Instead I ask if she was nervous. To get up on stage, all those people.

She has to confess to a little "reinforcement." Before leaving home, without my father seeing, she poured a thimbleful of scotch into an empty aspirin bottle.

I'm shocked. A nip before lunch? She should have offered me some. I catapult a paper clip across the room. She continues to question me—about the food, the seating arrangements, the color of the napkins . . .

What is this sheet of paper on my desk with words typed on it? I did not type them. Now I remember my mother hanging around the typewriter, gingerly touching the keys.

The words on the paper are: "Amerique. America. Maman I am here."

Traffic Manager

In the fantasy, my father comes to visit (at my invitation) and says to me, "I'm sorry. You were absolutely right." About anything.

About not wanting to sell my textbooks at college. About refusing to learn shorthand in order to become a secretary.

Then we speak of his childhood in Turkey, his forty-five-day voyage to America during which he subsisted on black olives and goat cheese and kept a diary (*Aujourd'hui la mer s'est calmée. J'ai mangé cinq olives mais il n'y avait pas de pain. Grâce à Dieu je me sens mieux.*) We don't speak of his terrible fury at me for wanting to keep the door to my room closed. ("Privacy? What do you need privacy for? If you want privacy, go to a hotel.") Or the day I wore an old coat on the street, thus showing the world that David Varon cannot provide for his daughter who should, for decency's sake, be wearing a bright red coat with brass buttons. My two brothers, for example—fathers now and community pillars—have never disgraced him. The question, What will people say? never arises. In this fantasy, not everything I do reflects on him. And when I voice disagreement, my parents don't feel my brow as though I've been plunged into a fever. No one says, "Perhaps you'll feel better later; have a drink of water" at those times when my anger splutters out, driblets of ineffectual rage, serving only to make me look ridiculous. "You are so much prettier when you smile," I've been told. And, "Is this what you learned in college, to be fresh to your parents?"

My father is a fervent believer, with tears in his eyes, in The American Way. All through my childhood, conclaves were held to discuss problems democratically: Should we go to Nova Scotia or the Grand Canyon on vacation? Do we want a green living room rug or a blue one? But: "You will not keep company with that person. Not over my dead body."

He drums on the table and sighs a good deal. "What's new?" he asks and repeats it ten times, not listening to the answer but still expecting it. Suddenly he will sigh deeply and say, "Everything's going to be all right," reminding me that unknown catastrophes are lurking.

"Did I ever tell you what my mother used to say?" he asks me as I reluctantly thumb through the *Reader's Digest*. "'Don't read too much, it will make you crazy.'

But it's nice as a hobby. My father was a learned man, he read all the French classics. '*Que diable allait-il faire dans cette galère!*'" he declaims. "Yessir," he sighs, "yessir, yessir . . ."

The *Reader's Digest* is better than no reading matter at all, although the feature titled "Laughter Is the Best Medicine" makes me slightly ill. But have I seen this? my father asks. He slaps the magazine. They've written about Victor Habib in "The Most Unforgettable Character I Ever Met." Look what a big fuss they made over him. The king of figs, a millionaire, and he can't even write his name. "I knew him when he had a pushcart on Rivington Street. The only thing he can write is checks. This man—you would not believe it [I would]—was the most unscrupulous, dishonest person. During World War II he traded in the black market, he did not pay his taxes, and now look at him. Two million donated to United Jewish Appeal, one million to Fresh Air Camps—and look at the rest of us."

For forty years my father has worked for Astra International Films, happy that he can call the president by his first name ("I knew him when he was in short pants"). Although he is an executive, the head of a large department, he fears making unreasonable demands on this billion dollar company, such as asking for an extra day's vacation. As a fighter for his staff, however, he is fierce. His "girls" (if they don't take advantage by dragging out coffee breaks or getting pregnant) know they can rely on him to ask for raises for them. The union is the culprit, corrupting his staff and making for inefficiency for which he gets the blame. Not to speak of the young punks who have taken over the company and don't know their ass from their elbow. " 'Listen John—' I call him John—I say, 'This is no way to run a company and that report is a lot of b.s.' I may not be educated," he says to me, "but I know what's right."

Fat lot of good it has done him, Mother and I say. "Forty years of blood, saving them thousands of dollars, and what have they done for you? A gold watch after twenty-five years, but would they ever pay your way to Cannes for the film festival?"

"It's a wonderful company," he says. "They have a good pension plan and they were among the first to hire Negroes. They make wonderful films." How would he know? He never goes to screenings but instead studies the box office reports lovingly. When he began there as a technician, the equipment was primitive; they worked with highly flammable nitrate film. He made splices by hand, my father did, using scissors and cement; never mind continuity as long as the film didn't break in the projector. Approached now by other companies, he has refused many opportunities to make a little cash on the side, fearing that it would be detrimental to Astra for him, David Varon, to accept a job expediting one film to a backwater in Bolivia. The commission would have paid for a dishwasher, I point out. "What do you mean? Your mother has nothing else to do all day," he laughs. "I wish *I* could stay home all day and relax and talk on the phone for hours."

When asked what kind of work he does, he stubbornly insists that he is the Traffic Manager. But for most people, traffic manager evokes the picture of a man in white gloves standing on a box in the middle of an intersection, rather than the administrator of foreign distribution.

How can anybody abide working for him? His instructions in malapropped English are infuriating because they are never complete. Each time he says, "I want you to type a letter for me," my hands turn clammy.

He has never said "please" to any member of his family—only to his superiors. My hesitation triggers his fury. "I ask you for a simple favor and you make a face. Is it so terrible to do your father a favor? You should get off your high horse and stop being such a snob."

On weekends he reads through the Sunday paper and drums on the table, waiting for Monday. "Everything is going to be all right," he says. "Isn't supper ready yet?" Then he opens the paper again, pointing out the Help Wanted ads for my benefit. "You see how much a secretary makes, an executive secretary. If you knew shorthand, I could get you a job with Astra." My father is a great believer in nepotism and Judaism. Why, I ask, does he want me to work for this rotten company that treats him so shabbily? It is better than being in a sweatshop, he says, and tells me the story of his friend Sol who came from the same small town in

Turkey and ended up being exploited by a pack of in-laws who ran a dress factory. An educated man. Which proves you shouldn't work for relatives, I say. Sol's wife was no good, my father says by way of explanation. She always wanted more and more.

"Materialism, the American way," I begin, but am warned by the catch in his voice. "This country is the greatest. We have everything here. Even people on welfare have color TV. I say anyone who wants to work—correct me if I'm wrong—" he interjects rhetorically, but fortunately we are saved by Mother summoning us to dinner. As usual, she has cooked as though all her children were still living at home.

Astra. With what shivers of delight did I see the Astra emblem flash across the screen at the end of some godawful film. It was the only thing I could ever report to my father that filled him with happiness.

Astra, this constellation of goodies, this garden of delights, begins to lose its old employees one by one, and my father hears the sound of the axe clearly. Perhaps they're right. He can't seem to keep on top of the work; he's falling behind. No one is indispensable, it's time to be ruthless. Nonsense, I say. After forty years (it's true that he's past the usual retirement age) they will give him an honorable release with severance pay and shares and consulting jobs.

"Those bastards," he says, "those young punks. If the father were still president, it wouldn't happen."

And when he is "separated" it is at the height of insurmountable confusion in his department. The computers have come; they have fouled up the records. "That ass, the treasurer, I almost told him to go F himself today." This is the first time he has used that initial in my presence. " 'What's the matter with you, Dave? The department is falling apart,' he says to me. If only they knew the truth, the incompetence of those bosses. I could write such an exposé—is that the right word?"

In addition, the personnel department has been pressuring him to hire the young man whose only credentials are recommendations from two probation officers. There is a strike at the airlines, the longshoremen are threatening, the prints of *Bandit Brigade* will not get through to Guadalajara. And a court case is pending over the toilet scene, so he is well rid of them, my father says, poring over the capsule summary of the new Social Security provisions in the *Times*.

It's all for the best, he says. Young blood, new methods. He, David Varon, is part of the great scheme of free enterprise called America.

"He needs a hobby," my mother wails, at his beck and call. He follows her around the house demanding to know who called and why. He reads the *Times*, but the *Reader's Digest* is late. Can't I find an excuse to have him come to my house, Mother asks. "Let him make phone calls from there, you are more centrally located."

"Maybe I'll take him to the zoo," I say to Mother and she says, "Yes, that might be nice, he likes being outdoors."

Every day now he puts on a white shirt and tie and finds an errand to do downtown: a loose end at Astra—he really hopes the company will collapse but wants to help his successor along because it's not the man's fault—a visit to the Medicare office. Do I (I!) know someone who could give him a job—Man Friday, Saturday, anything.

"Anything, anything," Mother echoes.

"What do you know," he snaps. "You don't know anything about business. Why have you bought so much fruit? You don't know the value of money." (Once, years ago, she indicated a desire to find a part-time job, but he was able to demolish her competence over and under the counter. He has always doled out the household money to her, and I have often been her co-conspirator, lying about the price of a purchase.) But he never stinted and we lacked for nothing. The trip to Canada, an electric typewriter for me, nothing but the best for his family. But now,"We can get along, thank God. No Atlantic City, that's all. Thank God Mother will be entitled to Social Security. I have a new health policy but it's fixed so the doctors make the money." Instead of a litany of complaints against the bosses, now I have to listen to an itemized balance sheet every time I speak with him.

One day I ran into him at an employment agency on

Madison Avenue. To him they said, "You are over-qualified, sir, a man with your experience."

"Well, honey," they said to me, "if you can't type more than fifty words per minute, you won't find a thing."

"You see," he wags his finger at me. "I'm not so dumb. I didn't go to college, but I know you don't get anywhere without skills. What do you mean, you hate it?" He laughs nastily and invites me out to lunch. I lie about a previous appointment. "I would rather go on welfare," I say, "than spend my life typing."

"It's people like you . . ." and the veins are beginning to stand out in his forehead. Please, not here on 40th and Fifth. And before he can accuse me of being an ingrate, why haven't I called home in a week, don't I care about my family, I'm so busy running around with bohemians—I leave, just walk away. And I wonder if he will go home and report that I was wearing a lackluster brown dress.

We celebrate his finding a job (through a relative, naturally) at one of those beastly family dinners in a mediocre chic restaurant. There is a great flurry of white-jacketed waiters of the same ethnic type, as though an entire Basque village had been imported for the occasion. A tree grows through the floor up into the skylight; pheasants strut freely in a glass-enclosed corridor that circles the restaurant. We have such dishes as *canard de Brest aux petit pois poivrés* and *consommé*

de tamarind à la mode de Beaumarchais and the obliga-
tory *crêpes flambées au beurre noir*, mostly misspelled on
the menu. Luckily, the strolling violinist is ill with the
flu tonight.

To be in a restaurant with my father means refusing
the table assigned to us, sending the food back several
times, and speaking about the personnel in French or
Spanish with the assumption that no one but our cozy
family understands. Mother, in the meantime, mutters
darkly about the superiority of home cooking.
Around us in varying degrees of familial agony are the
other diners. The candle on the table casts a murder-
ous light.

"That's great, Pop," my oldest brother says, quaffing
Grand Marnier as though it were beer. To him my
father never said, "Is this what they taught you at
college?" nor did he have to learn stenography.

Yes, my father says, he would have worked for nothing and so the piddling salary he will receive as some
sort of clerk is gravy, yes gravy. "And now we can give
you a dowry when the time comes." He sighs and
drums on the table.

The company for which he is privileged to be working deals in copper, rubber, cocoa, beans. An international trading company in which once again he feels
part of the vast scheme of progress. Happiness reigns at
home. No longer must Mother give a moment-to-
moment account of her whereabouts. He is *working* and
invites me to have lunch one day. No more lectures, I

say to myself. If I am working as a receptionist, it is because I like dealing with people ("Have I seen you here before, blondie?"). After all, what else is sociology good for?

He insists that I come up to his office on the twentieth floor rather than meet in the paneled Hickory House he likes so much, with its autographed photos of sports–show-biz luminaries, "the place where" (in a lowered voice) "the top brass bring their mistresses." I dislike the prospect of being paraded around as I used to be at Astra, dragged from one plush office into another to be introduced, but can't get out of it this time.

I have to laugh at the reception area, so like the one where I work. Pseudowood, pseudoleather, a kidney desk bereft of anything except a telephone, and real class—the old maps behind a glass display case showing ancient trade routes. I am directed—no, not that door, *that* door (the lady or the tiger?) to a hallway from which cubicles open on either side, with partitions frustration high, behind which you might pick your nose but not have a private conversation.

The clatter increases as the soundproofing abruptly leaves off, in mid-industry as it were, for I am now in the tropical products division. Also, I notice a distinct rise in temperature, as though the atmosphere has been designed to be compatible.

"Who?" they ask—the pimply office boy, the lacquered bookkeeper. "Oh you mean the new man."

Yes, I mean the new man, I suppose. Is his office this way?

"You mean his chair," the kid says. Okay, whatever it is.

"*Carborundum*," a gum-chewing voice announces over an unseen loudspeaker. "*Carborundum on seven.*"

And what is he doing when I enter his room? (No door; you knock on the door frame.) Reading the *Times*. He jumps up, puts on his jacket, and greets me. "Are you hungry?" he says joyfully. Without waiting for an answer, "Out gallivanting again?"

"I'm working," I say. "You know I have a job."

"Good, good," he says, pushing me outside. But I have seen the broken rung on the back of his chair, the impossibility of stretching out one's arms without knocking over supplies on the upper shelves. I've heard the transistor radio that drones incessantly from the cubicle next door, seen the grimy table stained with coffee rings from polyfoam containers. This is the mail room, doubling, I see, as the copy office and storage closet, with a glittering silver tray adding the right tone to the top shelf.

"Hey! Where are you going?" A man pokes his head out of a doorway as we pass. "Where's the stuff? I asked you for it half an hour ago."

"Right there on the desk, Mr. Nelson," my father says courteously. "I'm sure you don't object if I take my daughter out to lunch."

"Oh, is that your daughter?" That look. "I didn't

know she was your daughter. Have a nice lunch. Don't rush."

"You wouldn't believe the inefficiency in this place," my father says. "If I was running it—wait, I have to punch out." My *father* punches a time clock. "Wonderful thing," he says. "If they didn't have it, people would take advantage. They do anyway. They don't give me enough to do. I asked for more work and they said, 'Why do you want to knock yourself out? Take it easy.' Would you believe it? I wouldn't mind sweeping, it's good to do some manual work. I delivered something the other day to the Flatiron Building. You know, I've never been in it." He chuckles. "The man there—he couldn't have been much older than you—he gave me a tip, but I refused it of course." My God, he is cheerful. He slaps me on the back like a comrade. "It's wonderful, wonderful, no aggravation. I come, I go, no worries. I sleep at night. I'm lucky, lucky . . ."

He sighs as we go down in the elevator. He is the only man to remove his hat.

Feast of Lights

The car always knows, Mimi thinks when Richard phones from a service station. The last time Mimi's parents were to be picked up the ignition died. The time before that it was the radiator hose. The car knows. It works perfectly on all other occasions.

No, Mimi's parents don't mind, they say, when she phones to tell them of the delay. They understand, they'll wait, hours if necessary. With a car everything is easy and since they are being driven from their apartment on 86th and West End Avenue to Mimi and Richard's on 27th and Lexington, it will be no inconvenience, they are sure, for Richard to make a quick trip across the Queensboro Bridge to Astoria (by way of Flushing to pick up Mother's watch) so they can make a brief stop to visit an invalid aunt.

There is no time to balk, for Mimi's mother Blanche immediately says, "By the way, I am bringing five pounds of baklava. I had all those nuts and honey in the house and I couldn't let them go to waste."

Today's occasion, the Hanukkah party, brings together Mimi's parents and Richard's, the Tarikas and the Sterns, a meeting of east and west (Near East and West Germany). Richard's parents and his Aunt Hannah will come from Washington Heights in a taxi. The gifts for Richard's mother Lisl and her sister Hannah must be of equal value with a slight margin of permissible variation—a purse a cubic inch fatter, a necklace wider by a strand—to denote the difference in kinship. Richard's father is always happy with his ashtray or scarf.

All year Hanukkah looms large on the elder Sterns' horizon. Months in advance, Aunt Hannah plans the sweets she will buy for distribution on elegant plastic plates, one for each participant.

Wrapping the presents is always onerous for Mimi because the Sterns expect straight edges and unwrinkled tissue. But the paper always cuts ragged and Mimi is impatient with a ruler, even though she knows she is in for derision by Richard, who deplores her lack of care. Every time he straightens a picture on the wall she feels that some vital ligament is being strained. She knows too that he hasn't forgiven her for chipping a Rosenthal china soup bowl.

Torn between greed and contempt for the hypocrisy of their clean white shirts, the boys clump around in unfamiliar shoes. "It's illogical for me to clean up my room," Pete the elder says. "It's just going to get messed up again tomorrow."

"Don't give me any of that Talmudic reasoning, kiddo." Mimi picks up a dust ball by the tail and tucks it under the rug. "Bad enough they'll say something about your hair."

"It'll be worth it if I get something decent from them," Pete grumbles.

"You did," his brother Alex says. "I looked in the shower."

"Damn!" Mimi cries. "Can't we have any surprises?"

"Mommy," Alex says, "don't you always like what we buy you?"

"Of course, darling. You always know what I like."

Almost anything Mimi ever gave her own mother has found its way to someone else. The sweater she knitted appeared on Blanche's best friend, the blouse on the superintendent's wife. If Mimi brings cake to her parents, Blanche always says, "We have plenty. Take it home for the children." Blanche only dispenses. She's can't even go to a restaurant without carrying food in her purse.

"Here we are!" Richard's voice is raised in cheerful alarm, earlier than expected, warning Mimi from the intercom downstairs. Both sets of parents have met in the lobby. Mimi quickly empties the front closet, stuffing the down jackets and raincoats into the shower, behind the upended bicycles with ridiculous bows tied to their wheels. She fights the urge to alter the right angles of the living room chairs and pinches her cheeks so no one will say she looks pale.

In the outer hallway there is scarcely enough room for all of them, what with the fur coats and innumerable shopping bags. Mimi's father seems to be borne along off the ground, his cane pointing accusingly at her. He is flanked by his wife Blanche and Richard's mother Lisl, an honor guard addressing each other in opposing accents. Blanche has the soup for which Lisl has made the matzah balls, a historic collaboration like the Entente Cordiale.

Blanche Tarika is the heart's delight of her grandchildren, who can't understand the other grandmother's English. Lisl will surely exclaim, "Oh, *der Tisch ist so schön gedeckt*." The table looks so beautiful. Tables figure prominently in her cosmogony, and the Hanukkah table with its gifts piled high is the apogee.

The car ride with Mimi's parents, Richard tells her later, was everything he anticipated and more. Aside from his refusal to go to Astoria, there was the usual controversy on the best way to get to the East Side. Mimi's parents believe that Richard never takes a conventional route, a streak of perversity they recognize as typical of him. Moreover, Mimi's father insisted on reciting every street sign and giving colorful descriptions of the traffic lights while rhapsodizing on the amazing number of cars on the road, proof of America's supremacy in the world. ("What's good for General Motors is good for America," he often says.)

And Blanche wanted to take Third Avenue downtown even though it runs one way uptown. Before Richard could express his irritation, Mimi's father disarmed him with praise of the car, a twelve-year-old Chevy formerly owned by Aunt Hannah, who had given it to her nephew when she reached the age of vertigo and was no longer permitted to drive.

"For you, Mimi." "Take this, Mimi." "Mimi, here." Shopping bags, boxes, the heavy artillery of a friendly army advancing, all sights trained on Mimi.

"Please . . ." She holds her cheek to keep her smile in place. "One at a time. First the coats. In a minute, Aunt Hannah—yes, I see the package, give me your coat." Like a well-drilled company, they divest themselves at once, and Mimi finds herself weighted down with Persian lamb, muskrat, and mink, hoping her kids don't start their animal rights spiel.

Wavering between kissing the children first or commandeering the kitchen, Blanche chooses the latter. She'll see the darlings in their private quarters, away from the rabble.

In the kitchen she speaks to Mimi, sotto voce, in French. "*Comme ils ont engraissé.*" How they have put on weight since last time. Mimi smiles brightly at her in-laws, who hover near the kitchen entrance, not daring to advance.

"Yes," Mimi says, "yes," as her mother continues her comments in Spanish.

"Are you speaking Chinese?" Richard's father asks.

"Oh Max," Blanche laughs coyly, "you know we speak Spanish."

"Ah. *Cosi fan tutte!*" He escorts her gallantly into the living room.

"When do we eat around here?" Mimi's father says. "Sit down, sit down." He points to a chair with his cane, inviting his daughter to have a seat in her own living room.

Lisl Stern says to her daughter-in-law, "*Schätzchen, du musst* from *die Suppe* take off the cover or the *Klöse* will break." These are the famed eighteen-ingredient matzah balls over which a battle ensued at Lisl's mother's grave, where Lisl was accused by a cousin of stealing not only the jewelry but also this recipe. When Richard is at his most pensive about life and death, he speaks of the urgency of taking down the recipe from his mother.

Mimi returns to the kitchen in time to find Blanche firmly affixing the lid to the soup pot. Knowing how little it takes to trigger her mother-in-law's depression, Mimi explains what Lisl has just told her.

"Don't worry," Blanche says. "She's mistaken. I'll take care of it, you go inside and relax."

"No, you go. I'm the hostess, remember?"

Just then Lisl comes into the kitchen. "Ach, I thought I took it off. I made a mistake." The lid comes off again. She explains why, in intricate German, forgetting that Mimi can hardly understand her.

Mimi's father, who can't sit still, comes into the

kitchen tap-tapping his cane as though he were blind, which he is not, though he has other afflictions that prevent him from seeing. "*Was ist los?*" he snaps. "*Was ist los?*" the only German he knows. "Where's Richard? Why don't we all sit down?"

Richard and his father are in the study. Max examines every item on the bulletin board: outdated notices of neighborhood protest meetings, doodles by the children, quotes from Martin Buber and the head of the FBI, lists of figures indicating Richard and Mimi's precarious finances (though he can't know that). Max asks if Richard has seen the new Bulgarian cruise ship and the art deco exhibit. "Hello, sweetie," Max interrupts himself as Mimi offers him a drink. "Why doesn't she smile at me?"

"Later, Max," Mimi says. He is a darling. She herds the two men toward the living room. Max asks if they watched the six o'clock news.

"We don't watch the news on TV," Mimi says.

He stops in his tracks. "You don't watch the news? How is this possible? Don't you want to know what's happening?"

"Ever hear of the *New York Times?*" Richard asks.

"All the news that's fit to print," intones Mimi's father, aiming at the couch.

En route to the kitchen again, Blanche says, "With all due respect, these people don't know how to cook."

"Forget about it, Mom, please. If she wants the soup uncovered . . ."

"Mimi, Mimi—"Aunt Hannah corners her and forces a wad into her hand.

"No, what for? You already bought me a present."

Aunt Hannah's dress is almost a replica of her sister Lisl's. They swear they don't consult in the morning, but if Lisl is wearing triangles, so is Hannah. Aside from occasional beige or navy blue, solid geometry usually envelops both women. "This is special for you. You work so hard and you make everything so pretty."

As though on cue, Lisl is heard to exclaim, "*Der Tisch ist so schön gedeckt!*" obviously unaware of treachery in the kitchen.

"Mimi always does things so well," Blanche says.

"She takes after her mother," Aunt Hannah says with unbounded generosity

"She's a princess." Max kisses his daughter-in-law.

"Look how calm she is, what poise," Blanche says as Mimi dashes back and forth carrying platters to the dining table. "Nothing ruffles her."

Richard's parents and aunt shun the stuffed grape leaves, which they regard as pagan. The matzah balls arrive semidemolished. Though no one is blamed aloud, Mimi notices that Lisl is subdued for the rest of the meal. Afterward, Max lights a cigar and Blanche exclaims, "Oh, I can't breathe." She leaves to go into the bedroom where she will loosen her corset and put on Mimi's slippers. Blanche is considered something of a gypsy by Richard's parents, who change for dinner even amongst themselves, that *ménage à trois*. In all the fifteen years Mimi has been married, she has never seen Max without his jacket and tie. Only for her in-laws does she polish the furniture. For them alone does Richard maniacally strew the contents of his closet onto the bed in search of a respectable pair of pants. For her own parents, however, bright colors are sufficient.

It is almost time to light the Hanukkah candles and sing, Blanche's time to shine. She describes how the conductor of her choral group begged her to coach the others in Latin pronunciation. "'Who, me?' I said. They told me no one else could do it. It was exhausting, but what could I do? Imagine."

"I imagine," Mimi says.

"Many are called," Richard says, "but few have the sense to say no."

"Mother doesn't delegate authority," Mimi's father says. Translated into the vernacular this means that he resents her attending rehearsals or meetings.

During the lighting of the candles, Blanche outsings everyone else. *Her* Hebrew pronunciation is the correct one. *They* say "Oh-Maine" instead of "Ah-men." They say "*H*anukkah" instead of "Hanuk*kah*." Ours is the true accent of the ancients, she claims. How can she know? Richard challenges his mother-in-law. Maybe the ancients said "Oh-Maine."

Preposterous! Blanche laughs. How could they? There were no Germans then.

There were no Spanish Jews then either, Richard says.

"But this is how they pronounce it in Israel," Blanche says.

"Israel?" says Max. "They don't have religion in Israel. Only lemons."

"*Es war* very nice in King David's hotel," Lisl says, flexing her fingers. She is contemplating going to Tiberias for the waters because of her arthritis.

Peeking into the living room where Aunt Hannah has finished distributing the sweets, Mimi turns to Richard. "Oh really, the table is *schön gedeckt*," but he gives her a dirty look.

Next to each stack of presents are the plates filled with candies: miniature chocolate champagne bottles imbedded in rock candy, marzipan cigars and straw-berries, gold and silver chocolate-covered cognac balls, no longer available in America, but Aunt Hannah has connections in Yorkville—and marzipan peasant fig-ures with coins of the realm emerging from their rears. There are also bonbons—"bong bongs" as Richard's family pronounces it, jaw-breaking pfeffernusse from Germany (unlike their son, the Sterns never boycotted German products), and an orange for simplicity.

In the mayhem of ripping paper and exclamations, Mimi tries to postpone opening her gifts as long as possible. The children pretend to be astounded at the sudden appearance of two new ten-speed bikes in the living room, gifts from Richard's family. As they were instructed, they throw their arms around Aunt Hannah and kiss her, which does not prevent her from whispering to Pete, "You're welcome, sweetheart, but you should get a haircut soon, okay?" Lisl opens her purse and strews dollar bills over the heads of the children. As they scramble for the money, Richard says, "No, they got the bikes. We laid out the money. Hand it over, kids. Mama, *du musst* to me the money *geben.*"

"No difference," Lisl says happily.

"All in the family," Aunt Hannah agrees.

"Nothing is more important than family," Mimi's father says with a catch in his voice.

Savagely, Blanche tears the wrapping off her present, revealing a straw bag in all its peppery fragrance from the People's Republic of China. "*Oh, mais c'est merveilleux!* I can put my music in it."

Now, opening a large gift box, Mimi knows at once that the polyester print dress from the specialty shop on Fort Washington Avenue was never meant for a size seven.

"Perhaps if you take it up here . . ." Blanche is impressed by the label. "Or raise the waist or drop the shoulders."

"I have a dressmaker," Lisl announces. "Not expensive. But you don't worry, I pay. You come one day with me."

"We'll see," Mimi mumbles, while tearing open the next box. From Aunt Hannah an antique gold and pearl bracelet, far too large for Mimi's wrist.

"I have a jeweler," Aunt Hannah says. "Come uptown one day and I will take you."

It's hateful, the idea of giving up a weekday. Just

because Mimi doesn't have a nine-to-five job, these women will never abandon their efforts to drag her shopping with them.

Sweet Pete has given his mother a copper bracelet that he picked out himself from a vendor in front of Columbia University. "Goodbye, tennis elbow," he says, flushed with pleasure when she draws him to her.

"It's cheaper than acupuncture," says Alex, whose gift is a Mexican cookbook, a hint to his mother to jazz up her cooking. From Mimi's parents, a gift certificate from Bloomingdale's.

"I'll go with you one day," Blanche says. "I need help picking out a suit."

And Max loves the new recording of *Don Giovanni* which Richard will borrow and not return.

"God bless them," Mimi's father says, waving at the family. "Amen, amen."

Anxious to return to a more secular ambiance, Max asks Mimi if her ceramics exhibit has opened yet.

"What exhibit?" Mimi's father asks even though he was told about it a dozen times.

"She's so talented, my daughter," says Blanche.

"Do you get paid for that?" Mimi's father asks. "No? What's the good then?" He is trying to be respectful because of the others present. "Why don't you try to sell your work?"

"Try Macy's," Max suggests.

"They'll only cheat her," Mimi's father continues. He trusts no one. Everyone is a racketeer or a hoodlum.

He advocates public executions for those who spray graffiti on walls. "Sometimes," he is fond of saying, "I think the best government is a dictatorship." To which Blanche counters, "Some people don't believe in freedom," interpreting the U.S. Declaration of Independence in light of the number of times she can get away to rehearsals.

Max likes the president's wife. He saw her on a talk show. She is very sincere as is the president.

"Sincere!" Richard can't stand it. Sitting at the edge of the sofa and brandishing a nutcracker, "You think it's sincere to support terrorist African regimes?"

"Ah, Africa," Mimi's father says, trying for peace with honor.

"I'm from Africa," Blanche reminds her husband. "Alexandria is in Africa."

"It's funny," Max says, "you don't look African."

"Isn't he awful?" his grandson Alex whispers loudly.

"No politics, please," Aunt Hannah says, to Mimi's relief. In another minute her father would have asked Richard if he was a communist sympathizer since he once rooted for a Russian chess champion.

Seeing Lisl cover a yawn, Mimi takes Richard aside. "You're not driving them home."

"Oh no," Blanche says, overhearing. "We'll all take taxis." She wants to avoid a follow-up to the political discussion.

"You couldn't all fit into the car anyway," Mimi points out. She feels compelled to embroider. "There's something wrong with the signal lights."

"Really?" Her father is alarmed. "Richard shouldn't drive the car then, it's dangerous."

"It isn't dangerous, just a little risky." Mimi is feeling pretty reckless herself, seeing the end of the visit in sight.

"You should tell him to get it fixed. It's your responsibility."

"For God's sake, don't tell me my responsibility," Mimi says, helping him on with his coat. Her boys are snickering.

"I won't say anything," her father mumbles. "I'll be dumb. You try to help people and they spit in your eye." His grandchildren burst out laughing.

"Oh, cut it out," Mimi says to the boys, but she can't keep a straight face. "Actually, the signal is fine. It's really the brakes . . . No, I'm joking, where's your sense of humor?"

"Good Humor," Blanche says. "That's still the best ice cream."

"But Mom never buys it," Alex says, "because it's too expensive."

"Poor darling, Grandma will bring some next time."

"When?" Alex asks, salivating.

"Ring for the elevator, Alex," Mimi says sharply.

A slow exit with heavy shopping bags filled with gifts and sweets. Richard will go down with them and help get the taxis. "Everything was perfect," Aunt Hannah says, touching Mimi's cheek. "And the children behaved like little gentlemen."

"We had to," Alex says, "or she would have sent us to the Arizona Home for the Rude."

"Next time," Blanche whispers to her daughter, "cook the rice a little longer."

"Nothing like family occasions," Mimi's father says reverently. "Blood is thicker than water." He juts his face out into the air for the children to kiss and is last out the door, grasping his cane like a billy club.

"I always hear that," Alex says. "Blood is thicker than water. What does it mean?"

"It means we're stuck with each other," Mimi says. "Start carrying stuff into the kitchen, will you." She swallows Richard's leftover scotch even though a piece of parsley is floating in it.

"If we're stuck with each other," Alex says, "he should have said blood is thicker than glue."

"Personally I prefer rubber cement," Pete says.

"Not in your veins you wouldn't," his brother says, moving his finger experimentally through the sputtering flame of the last Hanukkah candle.

"That wasn't so bad," Pete says, handing his mother two leaning towers of glasses. "Some of my friends really hate their families."

Rafi

Lately Stella has been thinking about her childhood sweetheart. She can picture him so clearly up to the age of fourteen or sixteen with buck teeth, bony knees, and as skinny as they come—and then he's gone.

She hadn't thought about him for years until she went to the cemetery to check on her father's grave. Raphael's father's grave was adjacent to her dad's. What an irony that these two men who were not on speaking terms the last twenty years of their lives should now be inseparable.

No one told Stella that Raphael's father had died. Their families were very good at avoiding death. Don't talk about it and it will go away.

Seeing the graves of those two titans, cheek by jowl, Stella remembered how close their families had been ever since she was born, two months after Raphael. Ah Rafi, my boon companion, our mothers planned our marriage as they took turns pushing us in the same carriage down Fort Washington Avenue, their voile dresses blowing in the breeze from the Hudson River. Who knows, maybe I would still be married if you had become my husband. I heard you were roaming the Great Plains selling tax advantages to Middle America. You with your thirst for knowledge, your passion for art, an autodidact at twelve, determined to read through the *Encyclopedia Britannica* one entry at a time. If I were to see you on the street, I wouldn't recognize you. Can you still wiggle your ears? Are you still passionate about the photographs of Jacob Riis?

What is it about childhood that makes it seem like a happier time? Stella knows it wasn't. There was nothing dramatic like abuse or desertion—nothing like that. But Stella was a generally sour, nervous child, and ugly for sure. Timid too. God forbid that Stella should raise her voice or utter a criticism of a parent. That was almost reason enough to summon the family doctor to come and administer a "physic."

Still, she can remember childhood so much more clearly than yesterday's headlines or where she put her keys or whom she just spoke to on the phone. They say this is what happens when you age, though at fifty she's hardly in her dotage. Just enduring a divorce from a marriage she can hardly remember even though it lasted such a long time. So much easier to remember picnics in Palisades Park with Rafi and his family, ferry rides across the Hudson River, and sitting on the bedroom floor in his apartment with those leeches, their two kid brothers, playing "knucks," the lethal card game where you rapped the loser on the knuckles with the deck: "Knucks!" while their parents chatted in French, Ladino, English, whatever came to their lips. Those picnics . . . fields of wildflowers, no ticks then, the smell of lamb chops on the grill well before vegetarianism curbed their carnal appetites. Fifteen, twenty people, white flannels and straw boaters, all those polyglot friends from the old country, Turkey, Egypt, France, Greece. Everybody sang, Stella's mother played the mandolin, Rafi's aunt banged the tambourine, Cookie Haim went down on one knee and sang, "Are you lonesome tonight. . . ?" and the women sniffled. A little red wine, and everyone sang "Granada" to remind them of their long lost homeland in Spain.

Remember, Rafi, walking across the George Washington Bridge and putting one foot over the state line into New Jersey and keeping the other one in New York? Thinking of you also puts me in two places, the past and the present.

Stella and Raphael had lost touch. First their fathers quarreled and then, soon after Rafi's mother died, he moved out to get away from his father. Who could withstand the man's rages? Certainly not Colette, Rafi's mother, who could only manage a weak "*Mais, chéri*" when he railed against the laziness of his children and the corruption of government officials.

Occasionally Stella noticed blue marks on Colette's lovely fair skin and then Rafi would begin to shout. "*Ce n'est rien*," Colette would say in her soft Provençal accent. To this day Rafi has not forgiven himself for flunking French in high school and inflicting a different kind of pain on her.

When Rafi gave his eighteen-year-old son a video camera for his birthday, he thought about how much time had gone by since he worked in his father's photo and camera shop on St. Nicholas Avenue back in the fifties. He remembered how Stella used to come in on Saturday mornings to practice her French and keep his mom company in the front while he and his brother sweated away in the darkroom. If the union man came, the boys would pretend to be merely visiting their parents, and as soon as the man left they'd be back in the darkroom or perched on stools at the conveyor belt, clipping the envelopes onto a kind of clothesline and moving it along, or laying the black-and-white pictures onto a fabric conveyor moving them along to the drying drum. Thunderous machinery rolled all day, and a gas burner was used to dry the film rolls, even though it was 85 to 90 degrees in the summer. Fans blew the hot air on everyone. The fumes from the chemicals were deadly. In the rare silences when all the machinery synchronized for a breath, Rafi could hear his mother coughing and laughing at the same time at something Stella had said. After Rafi left home, he often wanted to call Stella or write but didn't know what to say.

When they were both around twelve, she told him about the birds and the bees, but she was talking about camels and polar bears because they had spent the afternoon in the Museum of Natural History. It had rankled that even though he was two months older he knew less than she. They were sitting on opposite ends of the couch in her parents' apartment from which you could see the George Washington Bridge. At age twelve and with an algebra final coming up, he could not quite make the connection between camels and humans. Another time she got him to kiss her, a first for both of them. Though what with her glasses and his buck teeth they made a clanking mess of it. For years after that, whenever he kissed a girl he thought of Stella as she was that day, tanned as leather, hair in black tendrils, a Pompeian fresco girl.

During his last trip, Rafi found himself thinking about his parents. There is a lot of time to think when you are driving across Kansas. Especially when you're heading for Denver to straighten out a mistake in your last sales report. Cheap bastards wouldn't pay his air fare. Dad was right after all. Never work for anyone else, be your own boss and keep the unions out.

When Raphael returned to his home just outside Salt Lake City, there was a letter from Stella. "Dear Rafi. This will come as a surprise after so long. I thought of you when I went to the cemetery to visit my father's grave—No, that sounds weird. Your dad is right next to him. Even in death our families are still close. Let's not wait until our kids put us underground to make a connection. Tell me what you're doing and what you look like these days. Are you still trying to learn the Kabbalah? Are you a grandfather?"

"Dear Stella. I will be in your territory next month." (*Territory?* she thought. Who talks like this?) "I heard you became a teacher. Good for you. I never went for a degree as you know, though I recently took a course on Buddhism at the local extension division (I'm looking into reincarnation). Life was my teacher and a pretty good one. If you want to know what I look like, here's a photo and article in the company newsletter. Most of what they say about me is b.s. but the picture is a good likeness. Do you still play shortstop?"

Is this my Rafi, this—patriarch—with the flowing beard and a trophy in his hand? *Congratulations to our own Raphael Nahmias. 284 units sold!* (Whatever that means.) No, the true Rafi is the scrawny kid who dragged me to the Museum of Modern Art when we were thirteen to look at the photographs of Henri Cartier-Bresson. Rafi, my surrogate brother, my betrothed from the age of one month, the hero who plucked a dragon fly (or "dining needle" as we called it) from my knee as I was picking daisies in a field. Not the sales associate who writes to me on company stationery.

Maybe Thomas Wolfe was right and you can't go home again. What can Stella be thinking of? Does she really want to hear about the Rotary Club and look at pictures of his children? Life must be very simple for him. He's bought into the American dream and all its values, all right. A company man—Rafi, who wanted to immerse himself in art and learn all about the greats of civilization. When he was in the army he sent a post-card from Japan saying he would have preferred to be in Europe to see the Renaissance, as though one could actually see a historical period, walk around it, take a picture of it.

Among all Stella's friends, then and now, Rafi was the only one who never criticized her, never passed judgment on her, always—like the Boy Scout he was—steadfast and true. Will he be shocked if she reminds him of the time they were at the bungalow in Long Beach and he asked to sleep in her bed—what were they, eight or nine?—and their parents laughed uproar-iously? Will he take it as a come-on, an attempt to tit-illate him? It titillates her.

Rafi was often mistaken for an elder in the Mormon church. Some of his best friends were Mormons. He didn't know if deep down they were really anti-Semites but he didn't care. His son was seriously dating a Mormon woman. Rafi never made a secret of his back-ground and was often asked to lecture before the local men's group because of his "Hebrew persuasion." His lodge brothers went to great lengths to establish a com-mon link between their different faiths. Rafi enjoyed being an anomaly in his town. Every Saturday he drove 60 miles to attend services at the nearest Jewish congregation.

When he was a kid back in New York he spent three deadening hours in Hebrew school every Sunday. Then he and Stella and the two kid brothers would all squeeze into the revolving metal subway entrance at 72nd Street, having paid one fare for the four of them, and ride home to Washington Heights. Sunday was the day of rest and chemistry experiments at his house. The stench of sulfur and the fragrance of *soupe à l'oignon* commingled as the four of them set about pouring and stirring and igniting their odd colored mixtures. Once there was an explosion and Rafi's father came storming in. Fire and brimstone! as Rafi's Mormon friends might say. Stella was so proud of one of her experiments, he remembered. Peel the shell off a hardboiled egg. Strip the membrane from inside the shell very carefully and lay it on a radiator to dry. A substitute for parchment if you were in a dungeon cell and needed to send a note. Most ingenious. He thought that she was brilliant, but she never lorded it over him, never made fun of him and his ignorance. If they did meet now, he intended to thank her for that.

It would be a sacrilege to set out to seduce a brother, Stella thought. She didn't want to scare him. Yet she knew that if he was her old Rafi, he would be ready to follow her lead while she wove her nets around him. She had often been unspeakably cruel and teasing to him when they were younger. Out of remorse, shouldn't she give herself to him? She didn't know his wife and it was better that way. Surely, surely, as a traveling salesman he'd had his encounters. Or was he that anachronism, the faithful husband? If he was, then time had stopped and he was a child still and her childhood hadn't died and true love still existed.

"A trip down memory lane?" Rafi asked as they walked past their old public school on Fort Washington Avenue.

"Please, no clichés." Perfect teeth, a big beard, but undeniably Rafi. They might have been continuing a conversation that started just moments ago. So as not to fall into temptation, she had urged that they go for a walk in their old neighborhood and hustled him out of her Greenwich Village apartment.

"Cliché, now there's a good word," Rafi said. He had recently learned that cliché meant "snapshot," which made a lot of sense verbally. "Remember the photo shop?" They were sitting in the park opposite the school, in view of the George Washington Bridge. "Child labor," Stella's father had called it, but how she had admired Rafi's skill at chopping the negatives with a hand cutter, working at lightning speed, never missing the fine line between each shot. Was it from the pictures of dogs, happy families, roses, and babies that Rafi had developed his love for the work of the great photographers?

"You were the one who took me to photo exhibits, remember?" she said.

"Yeah . . . but here's a great photo if you really want to see one." He whipped out a picture. She was hoping it wasn't going to be what she thought, but it was—a photo of his infant granddaughter. "Here's my cliché," he laughed apologetically.

"She looks like your father, I think."

"Fortunately, she doesn't have his temper like I do."

Stella thought of the two graves side by side. Two fathers who had been to school together in a little town in Turkey and emigrated to America on the same Greek freighter in 1930.

Rafi's father was the first in their crowd to own a car, but eventually Stella's father refused to ride with such a driver. That was probably the beginning of the discord between the two families. "*Pauvre Colette*," Stella's parents whispered. Poor woman, she is too good. Never discuss politics with him, Stella's father enjoined her mother, not politics, not labor unions, not the Allies' losses, not anything. Colette had lost family to the Nazis.

After Colette died, mysterious grievances came to light. Stella's father claimed that Raphael's father had once insulted a cousin of his when they were all living on the Lower East Side, before the young men had found jobs. Called her a "hoor" Stella's dad maintained, having put away the slight for future use. A few years after Rafi's mother died, his father became engaged to another woman. Stella's father refused to allow her to set foot in his house until he saw the ring on her finger. He didn't allow loose women into his home, he told Rafi's dad.

"I loved your mother," Stella said.

"She had plans for us." Rafi smiled, perhaps thinking of the wicker baby carriage they had ridden in together. Now the two of them would fit cozily in one bed, Stella thought.

She asked what his marriage was like. "Good," he said unhesitatingly, "though not perfect. If it were, we'd have nothing to work toward. I believe in working toward a goal, don't you?"

"Depends," she said cautiously, put off by his strategic planning approach.

"Being single seems to agree with you," Rafi said. "You look better than ever and I always thought you were beautiful."

"That's the first I hear of it." She could feel her face growing warm.

"I have a confession to make," Rafi said.

Now it would come, the declaration of undying passion, smoldering for half a century. She was ready for it.

"There's really no one else I can tell. I had an affair two years ago," he said. "I guess I just lost control. I was away, as I often am. It was a convention, she was alone there also. She had just given a terrific sales presentation—I picked up a lot of pointers from her. Anyway, there we were . . ."

"Yes, and here *we* are. These things happen." She faced him almost defiantly.

"I knew you'd understand," Rafi said. "You always understood so much. Taking her hand, he said, "I've missed you. I'm just—are you cold? Your hand is like ice."

She withdrew her hand and put it into her pocket where she could dig her nails into her palm without his seeing.

"I don't want to pry into your private life," he said after a moment, "but are you with anybody now?"

"I'm with you," she said, "sitting on a park bench."

He looked puzzled. "Did I say something to upset you? I'm not very good at reading people—except if I'm selling something to them."

"Yes, I noticed you got a company award." Safe ground again, but for how long? "The next time you come east, we might take in a museum or something. Did you notice that they've painted our bridge recently?"

He didn't speak for a moment and then he said, "In your letter you asked me about the photographers—you didn't mention Robert Capa, by the way—I don't have much time for wandering around museums. It would be a luxury for me. You didn't know about my son, did you? He seemed to show some talent as a photographer. We had him in a rehabilitation program. He was what they call a user, a fancy word for a drug addict. I hate fancy words. The only thing that saved me—you'll say I'm nuts—was listening to Wagner's *Ring Cycle* over and over while I was driving like a madman all around the country trying to do my job without letting on."

"Wait," she said, upset. "I'm trying to catch up." He was filling out, growing up before her eyes. She hadn't really known him after the age of eighteen. "I'm so sorry about your son." She laid a hand on his knee. "In answer to your question, no, I'm not with anybody now."

He took a deep breath. "He's my favorite of all three," he said, and she knew she'd lost her chance. "When I realized what was happening to him I almost lost my mind. My wife—you would like her, she's something like you." Kiss of death, Stella thinks. "She was amazingly strong through it all. She was a rock."

Now Stella begins to understand her loss over all those years, depriving herself of Rafi as a friend because she thought she'd outgrown him, and even until moments ago, judging him on the basis of his mode of expression and his profession. It's indecent enough to want to seduce him. Rafi's practically her brother. Blood brother, actually—as children they'd once jabbed their pinkies and mingled their blood. She isn't about to upset his existence now.

"What's wonderful is that I can tell you anything," Rafi says. "We're like best friends."

"Lifelong—and platonic." She tries to smile.

"I've always liked that word. I think of old man Plato sitting in that cave looking at the shadows on the wall, day in and day out. It's a great picture. I think there's a clue there somewhere."

Same sweet Rafi, still driven to find answers.

They part at the entrance to the subway, the one where they used to emerge in a cackling, silly group, pushing and shoving and hungry as anything.

Awkwardly he kisses her cheek. "Can we write to each other?"

"My pen pal," Stella says, giving him a hug and sending him on his way.

A Skirmish in the Desert

Ask my elderly mother how she is.

"When I see you we'll talk about the good things."

"Is something wrong?"

"All quiet on the Western Front."

It's the first salvo by the master tactician.

"Oh, my poor geraniums," she says.

"Why?" asks the innocent daughter, expecting a tale of horticultural woe.

"There's no one here to appreciate how beautiful they are."

I call upon my skills as a simultaneous translator, honed not at the United Nations but in a railroad apartment in upper Manhattan. The English translation of almost anything my mother says to me is: "You don't spend enough time with me."

Occasionally she crosses the no-man's-land of innuendo and reveals herself. "Don't you miss me?" she asks.

"I just talked to you yesterday."

"Talking is not seeing." This is a conversation worthy of Oedipus and the Sphinx. And why not? Mother was born in Egypt seventy-five years ago and she has always known the answer to the riddle of the Sphinx, namely, Never speak directly of painful matters. This is a precept instilled very early in the life of a Sephardic woman. Arabesques of hyperbole surround us from birth.

Here is my mother's account of a visit to a dying acquaintance. "I went to visit Angela on Saturday. First I took the Number 4 bus, then the 96th Street crosstown, and then I transferred to the Second Avenue bus. It went through terrible neighborhoods and it was very slow. But on the way back I took the bus that goes up Third Avenue, and that was fascinating. It goes through an Indian neighborhood. I felt like a tourist. At 66th I took the crosstown and got off at Lincoln Center. They are doing *The Student Prince* at the State Theater."

"But Angela—how is she?"

"It's better for you not to know."

Thus was I spared the news of the death of family friends, people who had known me as a child—whose funerals I would have wanted to attend, whose kin I would have embraced or written and who would probably always consider me bereft of feeling and common courtesy. My parents, when I confronted them time and time again, said they didn't want to depress me.

When an uncle of mine was in a coma, my father snapped, "He'll be fine, let's not spoil our dinner." Subject to the slings and arrows of corporate misfortune, he maintained that everything was going to be all right as long as it was not discussed at the dinner table. And yet there was menace everywhere: Speak to an insurance agent and you'll be cheated; if you go out at night you will be mugged; eat olives without bread and you'll get worms.

Health. Mother refuses to go to a doctor. She is afraid she'll be sent to a hospital where she'll become a learning experience for medical students and later will be left to rot. But why is she suddenly short of breath?

"It means," she said, "that a new sultan will be taking over."

Lady, this is America, this is New York. Hasn't she heard of the germ theory of disease, Louis Pasteur, or Alexander Fleming?

Here's one for the annals of medicine: King Fuad of Egypt visited the school for Arab girls where my mother was teaching. She was twenty at the time. Although she was the youngest teacher there, she was selected to make the welcoming speech. This she did in French, the language of choice for the educated people. Then the king spoke. But he could not really speak, he could only bark. It was very sad but everyone had to keep a straight face. The girls were very well-behaved. They were the daughters of wealthy

Arabs to whom little was denied—clothing, baubles, entertainment, education—even though they would end up like their mothers, heavily swathed in veils and accompanied by bodyguards and chaperons as they rode around Alexandria in their family limousines. But we were speaking of beloved King Fuad, father of the playboy heir apparent, Farouk, whose palaces guarded both ends of the boulevard that ran along the sea. King Fuad, my mother says, had an operation in which he received a liver transplant. The liver had come from a dog. Hence the bark.

History. "We always lived in harmony with the Moslems," my mother says. "It's only since Israel that there have been conflicts." History tells us otherwise, I point out. There were fierce massacres under the reign of the Almohades. And the Koran says that if the Jews have not converted to Islam after 500 years they must be wiped out. Under the Moors we had to wear distinctive clothing that set us apart from the Moslem populace—one red sock, one yellow, for example.

"I had many Arab friends," she says, puncturing my history lesson.

"Abou Ben Adhem," she announces, and I know a performance is imminent. She has a special fondness for the Leigh Hunt poem that she learned at the Lycée in Alexandria. As she recites the oratund syllables, you can almost see old Abou Ben Adhem ("may his tribe increase") dozing over his letters until he is startled by

a vision. Mother's eyes flash and her hands conjure up
the angel writing in his book of gold. And since
"exceeding peace had made Ben Adhem bold," he
asked the angel what he was writing. Why— "the
names of those who love the Lord." I knew what was
coming: Poor Abou's name was not on the list. But
Mother, backlit by the sun going down over the Jersey
Palisades, brought the angel back, and this time—
"Lo!"—Ben Adhem's name led all the rest.

Religion. Unbeknownst to my father, my mother sang
in praise of Jesus Christ. He knew she sang with a
choral group that performed in Carnegie Hall several
times a year. Not being a classical music lover, he never
attended the concerts. Masses, cantatas, requiems, Te
Deums—she sang them joyfully in her vibrant alto
voice. At first she only mouthed the name of Christ
but it threw her off tempo. God would excuse her for
singing Bach and Mozart, might even give her points
for it. She once, only half jesting, expressed the wish
to be celebrated upon her death with Beethoven's
"Missa Solemnis."

Her religiosity has always been flexible. I, her
daughter, must not sew a hem on the Sabbath, but
God would forgive her for going to Lord & Taylor in
search of a raincoat.

When I paid a rare visit to the synagogue for the first
annual commemoration of my father's death, she
provided a running commentary on Mrs. Franco's

marital troubles, the Sarfaty girl's weight, the wealth of Matarasso's widow. The eternal light shone balefully at us from the Ark below, where the men were sitting, and the sexton in a top hat frowned at the chatter from the women's balcony.

A few years earlier, prevailed upon to attend a reception for a visiting Israeli diplomat, I said to my father that I did not want to sit next to the rabbi. During a wave of virulent apartheid activity, this cleric had made me a personal promise to issue a public statement condemning U.S. support of the South African government. Week after week I waited for news of the sermon, but it was not forthcoming so I stopped attending synagogue altogether.

"Why won't you sit next to him?" my father asked.

"Because he'll say he hasn't seen me in a long time."

"So be frank with him," said my father.

"What do you mean?"

"Tell him it's because you go to another synagogue."

Miracles. I learned of the suicide of Albert Delburgo, my father's friend, quite by accident. I overheard a family friend say that it was his punishment for having married a Christian woman. Intermarriage and divorce were classified as scandals in our family, along with expecting repayment of a loan by a relative, and taking your trade to an outsider when a relative was in the business.

At the memorial service, which was attended by Albert's widow, Dorothy, a flutter of wings was heard under the high-domed ceiling of the synagogue. A dove had found its way into the holy edifice and was flying about, its shadow crossing the stained-glass windows. A dove, not a pigeon. And therein lay the miracle, according to Dorothy: It was the Lord's forgiveness to her husband for having left her bereaved. Even my mother was impressed. She didn't approve of inter-marriage but she had a healthy streak of superstition. She invited Dorothy to her home for the first time, an invitation that had been withheld during Dorothy's ten-year marriage to my father's friend.

"We also have miracles," my mother said while serving us coffee and sweets. She reported that in the Middle Ages there was a woman messiah from her own country, Egypt. "Yes, a woman, no less." She sat back with satisfaction as though she were the incarnation of that strange female but was waiting only until the world showed itself worthy to receive her.

"If memory serves," I said, calling upon history once again as my sword and shield, "she was just a screwed-up teenager and was denounced by the rabbinical authorities. There were reprisals against the Jews, and more got themselves burned at the stake than was usual for that time of year."

"Where would you be if not for the Inquisition?" my mother demanded. "Do you think you would be here today, a college graduate, a liberated woman?"

"Another miracle," I said. "Thank you, Torquemada."

"We left Spain and went to Turkey," my mother

continued, turning conversationally to the widow Dorothy, as though recounting her latest package tour instead of the wanderings of our ancestors.

"It was a miracle that you were spared," Dorothy said fervently.

"You see?" Mother says pointedly.

Now there's a tweeting of birds on the windowsill. The three of us turn. There are several sparrows chirping hysterically. "They must have smelled my cookies," Mother says fondly.

Secret weapons. Strategy involves the movement not of troops but of casseroles, from my mother's home to mine. Communiqués from the field are couched in solicitude. The daughter has a slight cold? You must rest, stay in bed, do not go to work, remain supine so I can conquer you with consommé. Thus will the short-term battle be won.

In the meantime, I wait for the signs of infirmity in her that will allow me to take care of her, but Mother seems to have confounded nature.

Her finest hour comes decked in historical trappings that even I find unassailable. An erudite cousin discovers an illustrious ancestor who wrote a treatise on morals in the sixteenth century in Safad. The item in the *Encyclopedia Judaica* has made its mark. "That's who I take after," my mother says. "You see, we have the same family name." The Xeroxed copy sits in the best frame that Woolworth's had to offer. "No wonder," she adds.

"No wonder what?"

"No wonder the Sephardim are considered superior. Even the German Jews know it. And they think they're better than everyone—except us."

She is speaking of her German neighbor, elegant Mrs. Oppenheimer, whose husband died in the camps. Unlike my mother, she never appears at her door in a housedress and slippers. Perfectly coiffed, nails polished, she is ready for a coffee klatch promptly at four o'clock every afternoon, but one must have an appointment.

Not only is my mother the commander, she is also the mess sergeant, ready for hungry armies any time of day or night, contemptuous of those who, like Mrs. Oppenheimer, will be thrown into confusion if there is a ring at the door except by prearrangement.

"It's in the blood," my mother says. She is speaking of our illustrious genes, about which we were recently informed at a cousin's wedding. The officiating rabbi spoke of our sixteenth-century ancestor and said that since "parenting" was the end-all of marriage, it was fortuitous that this illustrious strain had made its way into the bride's "gene pool." I looked at the bride closely. She was an account executive at a major advertising agency and wore her hair in the shaggy mop mode. The rabbi further revealed that you don't have to be Jewish to want children—a concession to the many young gentile guests.

"Yes, the blood," my mother says again. "You will

inherit it all when I'm gone," she adds, her notions of genetics being somewhat hazy. "Did you know that I had a stillborn child before you were born? And then a miscarriage when you were just a baby? Both boys."

I'm shocked. "I had no idea." It's the first time she's sharing privileged information with me.

"I always wanted a daughter," she says, sealing her victory with a kiss.

Changelings

The children correct each other's manners at dinner. With his elbows planted on the table as demarcation points of his territory, the fifteen-year-old says, "It's really disgusting the way you eat."

The younger boy lifts his mouth from the rim of his plate. "You're no model of couth yourself," he says.

His brother shoots a pellet of bread at him and leaves the table with a curse.

"Watch your language," I say automatically, because a response is expected of me by the younger. I would give up, wear ear plugs, or eat alone if I could. But left together they would quarrel more violently.

I listen now as the younger one, Rick, goes into his room. The inevitable occurs. A loud kick of a sneaker against the outside of his door.

"Get out! I told you to get out. Get out, Jess. Ma! . . . Ma, he's in here. . . . Get out!"

I rush in before blood spills. Rick is alone. The other one is in his room. What was all that yelling?

Rick flips a switch. "*Get out, get out! I told you . . .*" It is a message on the tape recorder. If he wanted to, Rick explains, he could rig it to work the moment the door is kicked or opened.

I knock at Jess's door, then walk in. Through the mesh of his gerbil cages and the forest of drum stands I glimpse something moving like a snake, the telephone cord.

"Yeah, what?" he inquires. He is lying in bed with the receiver form-fitting his face. One must make an appointment to speak to him between calls. He has managed to figure out the abstruse tables in the telephone book and assures me that he is on a one-message unit that is good for three hours.

I explain—between interjected comments to his friend: "Yeah, my mother. Ha ha. Shut up—" instructions I have for him pertaining to the yogurt. Since he will be up later than I, because this is Friday night, no school tomorrow, will he please unplug the machine at a designated hour and refrigerate the jars. For a while I was making yogurt the way my grandmother used to, on top of the radiator, but the children made fun of me and pooled their resources to buy me the machine.

It occurs to me now that almost all my conversations with Jess deal with food: You skipped breakfast again? Did you eat the school lunch? It seems to be the only safe subject. (I wonder what his father talks to him about when Jess visits.) If I ask him to be home by a certain time, I am ruining his life, have no trust in his judgment. And if I offer to buy him a reading lamp, he says not to bother, he won't be living here much longer. After all, as he reminds me, my own father left home as a teenager and traveled clear across the world in the hold of a stinking ship.

Rick, I think, expects to spend his declining years within the bosom of his family. Unlike his brother, he prefers staying close to home, especially in the evening. Is he fearful, or does he want to spare me the agony of waiting up? Rick will do anything to avoid a scene. Jess thrives on them.

"I won't be home tonight," Jess says half into the receiver. Is he talking to me or to his friend? I turn to go.

"Where are you going? I just told you something and you turn your back."

I ask if he is on or off the phone, and naturally he says, What is the difference (his friend must be enjoying this), he is speaking to me.

"And I to you," I say, wanting to wrest the instrument from him and pull it out of the wall. But with his rages he is capable of breaking my arm. He towers over me, his shoulder-length hair giving him a savage look, the acne like decoration before a battle, new stubble like protective covering on his child's skin.

At last I learn that he plans to hack around and boogie with some friends. "Why don't you speak English?" I say before I can stop myself.

A string of four-letter words hits me. "See, that's English. Means nothing. Just pure bull. Why should I have to talk differently to you than to my friends?"

"Because you must be Ernest in the city and Jack in the country," I say, taking refuge as I always do in what he can't know. This is the same child who listened raptly when his grandfather described the custom of kissing the hand of a parent to show respect.

Jess is planning to go sledding tonight in Riverside Park, which is covered over with ice. Riverside Park even by day is an unlucky place. "The park at night?" I say.

He will be with friends. Besides, the muggers don't go out in winter because they haven't got warm clothes.

In the dark—on steep ice? "One could be killed," I say, my voice rising.

"It's all settled," he says. "Don't worry. I'll be careful."

Elaborately I tell him how much faith I have in his good sense. Nonetheless—but what's this? He is fixing the steering mechanism of the sled.

All it needs, he says patiently, is a couple of new screws. Reluctant to display my ignorance, I say nothing. They already think me quaint because I blanch when I hear such terms as "running a wire" or "tripping a circuit." I once woke them in the middle of a thunderstorm and made them put on their sneakers so they would be grounded in case of lightning.

Perhaps Jess is right. Sledding can't be more dangerous than walking on the street at night in balmy weather.

Aware that I have no chance, I say to him, "I just want to go on record as telling you that I don't want you to do this. It is dangerous and I am worried."

"I don't know what you're talking about," he says. "They're all waiting for me. They need my sled."

He goes into his room and makes a call, forgetting to close his door. "Yeah, isn't that dumb, she says it's dangerous. What's playing at the Loews? . . . Maybe you can convince her." He calls me. His friend would like to speak to me. I decline.

He makes another call. I don't want to hear it. Finally he comes out, zipping up his parka. I notice the sled is no longer in the hall. Can I assume that he is actually obeying me?

"I'm very glad," I venture. "That's the smart thing to do."

"I just want you to know," he says, "that you have made me thoroughly miserable. I hope you're satisfied."

"Go to a movie," I say. "I'll treat. Eat something later." I rummage in my purse.

"I don't want anything from you," he says and leaves.

I know he is short of cash. What will a boy do if he needs money? *We're holding a teenager here who says he's your son. We picked him up for soliciting.*

I go into Rick's room. He looks up from his graph paper. "Another fiendish contraption?" I say, concentrating on his design.

Would I like to see how it works? he asks. He is my young Thomas Edison, comfortably seated in an old wooden swivel chair facing a massive oak desk from the Salvation Army. He loves old things. He has boxes filled with old candy wrappers and missing bits of toys. One never knows when they will be useful. He describes to me how, with a pulley system and gears, a skateboard can be made to accelerate without one's having to push on the ground with the foot. The idea came to him because Jess was complaining about his inability to accelerate uphill effectively. "See, Mom?" he says, his voice cracking. "Did you understand?"

"Perfectly," I say, kissing him. His grandmother, my mother, believes he is a genius because he can fix anything. For her all mechanical devices are inhabited by spirits, amenable only to those with special powers.

And what is he doing this evening? I ask, knowing that the thought of leaving his cozy nest is anathema to him.

"Oh, I'll do a little bit of this and that," he says.

By which, I think with sudden irritation, he means television, many hours' worth.

"This room is a mess," I say suddenly. "I've asked you time and again to clean it up." If he is staying home, he must pay the price.

He is too much the homebody, too fearful of walking a block to a friend's house. He will never be prepared for life because I shipped him to nursery school before he was ready. It was the children or me, and I chose wisely but unwell. He refused all food at the school and was made to rest along with the other tots for three hours every afternoon. How could I know? The colors were cheerful, every child had an individual cubby.

Why doesn't he go and visit his friend David who lives in the building, I suggest.

"You just told me I have to stay home and clean up."

"That can be put off if you have a date," I say, self-defeating as usual.

"There's nothing to do there," he says.

"Invite him over here then."

"There's nothing to do here."

I leave him to his devices. I know that once I am in bed he will quietly turn on the TV channel that shows porno movies, the sound low so I won't hear. Sometimes when I am out during the day and come home, I see his shadow quickly crossing the French doors of the living room and I know he has been watching TV in the afternoon. Aha, I will say. Caught you. I was practicing piano, he says, his face flushing. And indeed there on the piano is his music, open at the right page. He thinks of everything.

Now the house is quiet and I begin the wait for Jess. Until tonight I could always count on his calling if he planned to be later than midnight (how he always found the right coin and an operable phone never failed to amaze me). Tonight he is probably saying to his friend, "She doesn't really care about me, she just wants to impose her life-style."

At two minutes past twelve he calls. I am enchanted with the grunt that passes for hello. Not to worry, he says. He and his friends are really getting down. I know enough to realize this means something good. He promises to take a taxi home. Then he asks how I am. I tell him to have a good time. He seems reluctant to get off the phone. "What's new?" he asks. "Since I saw you last, not much," I say, laughing. "Don't worry," he says again. He has money. He ate something. He won't make noise when he comes in.

In spite of myself I do fall asleep before he comes home.

In the morning I awaken with a start. My first thought is, did he come home? I open the door to his room very quietly. There is a form on his bed. I see corduroy legs sprawled out, a boy in a sweatshirt. Poor thing, he was so tired he had no time to undress. I approach the bed. The little I see of the face is contorted, the hair wild. My God, did he get stoned last night?

The child wakes up and lifts his head to look at me. It looks like Jess, yet not really.

Suddenly I realize that it is not Jess, it's another boy.

"Where is Jess?" I ask with terror in my heart.

The boy looks at me with glazed eyes.

I run out and fling open the living room doors. There on the couch in his sleeping bag is my boy. I see now what happened. Passing Jess's room again, I notice a note taped to the door. *Dear Mom. My friend Michael is sleeping in my bed. I am in the living room. Love, Jess.*

His friend Michael, in spite of his ferocious appearance, tremblingly sits up in Jess's bed and in Shakespearean English apologizes for his disarray and any perturbation he has caused.

I am so happy this morning. I will prepare a mammoth breakfast for all these fine boys. Ordinarily a sluggard, Rick has taken it into his head to precede me into the kitchen. The table is already set, and I find him folding paper napkins into swans.

Silver Screen

It should not have come as a surprise to learn that Victor Hattan had been impersonating his son. What is a retired seventy-year-old widower to do when his son is incapable of conducting the business of life?

In the Hattan family, the son was prized far above the two daughters. But try as he might, Jerry Hattan never measured up. Victor saw to it that this was not known outside the confines of the family. In the Hattan way of life, dissembling was instinctual and circumlocution the language of the people. Even simple requests were camouflaged: "It seems to be getting dark" for "I want you to get me a snack, preferably something sweet, accompanied by a glass of milk, not too cold." The rules of discourse were strict, and members of the tribe knew them well. You entered the tent or condominium and delayed stating your business. First, there was the ceremonial small talk and refreshments, and

inquiries into the health of the reigning sheik—Victor—
then discussion of the deplorable state of the union,
and finally, through a few discreet phrases, the facts
were unfolded. Reality thus glided in through the
service entrance.

So first there was the traditional culture that forbade
the direct statement. Then there was Hollywood.

Although Victor actually visited the place only once,
it consumed forty-five years of his working life.
Hollywood pervaded the Hattan home. It was the source
of the glossy photos of movie stars on the daughters'
bedroom wall during their teens, the source of their
daily bread and of the glamour the Hattan children
thought was theirs because Victor worked for Polaris
Pictures International, even though he was at the distribution end in New York City. His job was to bring
nirvana to the masses, mainly in South America.

Everyone dreams of finding the perfect match between a job and one's temperament. Victor had already
been trained at home in the techniques of illusion—the
illusion that nothing is amiss, that relatives don't fight
(though it is permissible for them not to speak for a
number of years), that everything will come out all
right. The fact that he fell into motion pictures as a
profession was entirely fitting. Here too he dealt in
perfect people and happy endings.

His role in the industry was a humble one at first.
Without benefit of sophisticated editing equipment, his
job was to cut a finished feature film down to the size

required by a given country as though it were a piece of yard goods, with no need to match up the pattern. Peru demanded one hour, Uruguay, one and a half, Panama, being miniscule, three-quarters of an hour. This kind of editing required no formal training. In his spare time Victor assisted his brother Daniel, who was engaged in another aspect of film, the creation of optical effects—more illusion—and the magnification or shrinking of the image.

Later Victor rose in the corporation to become assistant vice president for foreign distribution. High box office figures for the latest Polaris Pictures film brought joy to his heart, and he would come home boasting about "our picture." But unless summoned by a higher authority, he never went to any screenings of Polaris's films, relying solely on *Variety* and the comments of others for his opinions. He was simply too restless to sit through any kind of performance. Victor revered the company for giving a poor Jewish boy from Turkey a job where he could become an executive, without a college education.

Polaris's logo he equated with the Statue of Liberty, even though the curvaceous figure of a starlet holding a rainbow was a far cry from the lady in the harbor. Still, to Victor, they both symbolized democracy in America.

How happy he would have been had his son learned something of the film business. Barring that, he would have been happy if Jerry had learned to be a shoemaker or anything else that would have given him a trade. For the young man drifted from one job to another, squandered money, put on weight, and still lived at home. From childhood, as the son of a Sephardic family, he was touted as the person who counted most (after the father), yet disappointed time and again. Very early on, Victor took to paying his son's bills and handling his bank account.

Jerry's enthusiasm for the latest postmodern architecture, his passion for such heroes as Lord Nelson or anything to do with the Nile—even his volunteer work at a senior citizens home—merely irritated his father. What good was it to receive glowing letters from relatives of these aged men and women with whom Jerry spent hours, listening to their stories, wheeling them about the terrace, and commiserating about the cold-heartedness of their children? "Everyone takes advantage of him," was Victor's refrain. "He's too soft. He needs to toughen up."

Victor's remedy for Jerry's lack of gumption was to supervise his every action. At the dinner table he watched closely as Jerry picked up a water pitcher, and never failed to admonish him to be careful lest he spill some water, and invariably Jerry did spill it. He had the family so well programmed that, even as children, Jerry's sisters were always prepared when the fork dropped or the plate broke. Jerry was Victor's creature, taking on, as he entered his twenties and then thirties, Victor's mannerisms, his stoop, his imperious gestures, his slight accent, even though the son was born in Manhattan and not in Istanbul.

It was as if Jerry might finally begin to please his father by acquiring his characteristics. But the bills continued unpaid, the health coverage lapsed, so Victor took it upon himself to play the part of his forty-year-old son, easy enough for a man who had lived, however vicariously, among actors and actresses and who preferred not to be a mere spectator.

He became convinced that Jerry was being evasive whenever he questioned him, which he did often. Why had Jerry suddenly run out of money? Why couldn't he pay his dental bill? What happened to the life insurance policy Victor had purchased for him?

"I cashed it in," Jerry said. "I needed the money."

"For what?" Victor asked.

"I had expenses," Jerry maintained.

"What kind? Tell me," Victor said wildly. "I wouldn't care if it was a woman, if you had gotten her into trouble and she needed money for an abortion. . . . Whatever happened to that widow you were seeing—is she the one?" He was going mad with conjecture, but no more information was forthcoming.

"I wish he had a mistress," Victor later confided to his eldest daughter, now safely married in Boston after an on-again, off-again affair. He had come a long way from the days when a sexual liaison scandalized him.

Posing as Jerry over the phone, he had attempted to find out more from the insurance company but was unsuccessful. The policy had been suddenly terminated and the cash withdrawn, and that was that.

"Where's the harm?" Victor demanded when his younger daughter Susie caught her father in flagrante delicto, having stopped by unexpectedly (she had her own keys) to find him speaking on the phone with an officer at the bank where Jerry had an account. She heard the tail end of the conversation in which he said he was calling merely to verify his balance, having misplaced his bank statement. Jerry had claimed to have a certain balance in his account and Victor seemed almost disappointed to learn that he had been telling the truth. His first thought was that the bank officer and Jerry were in collusion, that Jerry had really withdrawn half the funds and spent them either on a woman or on horses and that the banker had gotten a cut.

"How can you do this?" Susie spluttered. "Pretending to be another person? If nothing else, it's illegal," she added, her indignation bolstered by her newly acquired status as a member of the bar.

"Are you going to send your own father to jail?" he asked.

"But suppose he finds out?"

"He would be grateful," Victor said. Whatever he was doing was for Jerry's own good, he explained, as though his daughter were feebleminded.

In despair over Jerry's deficiencies, he even considered paying for the services of a psychologist so long as there was a guarantee of immediate results. "On the

other hand, a trip to the mountains can do wonders,"
he mused. After all, to undergo psychotherapy meant
that one was crazy, and this he could never countenance in his own family. He called some trusty advi-
sors: the rabbi of his synagogue, the head of his congregation, and the administrator of Polaris Pictures'
pension fund, for guidance "on behalf of a friend who
is worried about his nephew." Only the head of the
congregation confirmed the salubrious effects of a trip
to the mountains; it had cured his niece's obsession
with a Pakistani engineer. Hearing this—Victor's cover
having been blown, he was keeping Susie up to date—
Susie suggested he send *her* to the mountains, preferably the Alps, but he waved her off. She was not worth
the bother.

When Jerry was fired from yet another job, Victor
muffled his voice and telephoned the employer to ask
for a clarification of why he had been let go. The
employer, the owner of a small jewelry business, erupted. "Are you out of your mind? You think I'm going
to hang onto someone who is filching watches from
the moderately priced line?" When asked to put this
damning evidence in writing, the owner cursed and
hung up, which made Victor spring to the conclusion
that the man was lying through his teeth, as he told his
daughters. In a major reversal of Sephardic cultural
policy, he was giving them current bulletins of all the
bad news. To deflect the impact of Jerry's wrongdoing
on her father, Susie the lawyer pointed out that the

owner probably did not want to become entangled in possible legal proceedings. "Bosses are all crooks," Victor said with satisfaction, having found his own screen against the truth.

Susie couldn't bring herself to tell Jerry all of what she now knew, but she did warn him not to be surprised if their father was acting in a rather unusual fashion—on Jerry's behalf, of course. "To be blunt," Susie said, "he's been making calls, using your name. Go easy on him, he's old—"

But she needn't have worried. Jerry shook his head in wonder at his father's audacity. "What a card he is," he said proudly. "I have to give him credit." Then he asked if she had caught the latest exhibit at the Metropolitan Museum.

"I know you would not steal," Victor assured his son during one of Susie's visits.

Jerry nodded—whether in agreement or in appreciation of his father's detective work, Susie couldn't tell. He said nothing.

"If you did steal," Victor went on, "there must have been a reason," stretching rectitude to fit his wish and thinking perhaps of *Les Misérables* (the book).

Jerry rose to the challenge. He told a story that would have done credit to the Screen Writers Guild, about being waylaid on a dark corner, about extortion and blackmail because of the widow he had been seeing who, he knew now, had connections to "Cosa Nostra." He smiled when he said this and turned to Susie.

"That's mafia, you know. Like *The Godfather*."

"Great movie," his sister said. "Did you go to the police?" She was falling in with this scenario.

"No, no," Victor said hastily, "that would be a mistake. Think of the publicity. We would be disgraced." As though this would be front page news in the *New York Times*. "Think of public opinion [a.k.a. Uncle Daniel]."

"We'd get a bad review," Susie said.

"Exactly," he concurred. There must be no taint on the family. Jerry's aberrations must never be revealed to the outside. Besides, what was wrong with spending money? That's what young men did.

Ah, his son, his son, a chip off the old block. The last bill had been paid off. Victor was now perusing the want ads on behalf of Jerry and had even sent off a letter of inquiry in his name. He was working on a résumé and cover letter and was coming to his daughter Susie for help with spelling. However, he would not listen to her advice. One could not say, "*I am honest and reliable.*"

"How else will they know?" asked Victor, "unless you tell them?"

Jerry approved the text of the letters, made a few emendations and signed his name. He was enjoying this collaboration. It was one of the few times when there was total harmony between the two men.

Behind Victor's efforts was the fear that no one would look after his son when he himself was gone.

He wanted him to be independent, he told Susie. He wanted him to learn to stand on his own two feet, which was unlikely, she thought, so long as her father continued to pull the ground out from under him.

Unemployment insurance was running out for Jerry, as it had so often before. It was high time he found work again, Victor said. Anything—stuffing envelopes—so long as it was steady.

Such a job was not what Jerry envisaged. His tastes ran more to being an amanuensis for a diplomat (Jerry's smatterings of foreign languages would be an asset) or serving as assistant to an antiquarian book-seller, or even being a concierge in one of those hotels that catered to Europeans.

Victor was the one who opened the replies from prospective employers. And it was he who phoned to make appointments for interviews, sometimes without consulting Jerry. Invariably these interviews did not pan out; presumably, the gulf between the application and the applicant was too great.

"He has no confidence," Victor observed and again reminded Jerry to stand up straight. At one time, the younger man had been a head taller but now father and son seemed almost the same height. It was as though Victor was draining some of the youth from his offspring. Jerry's accent seemed to grow more pronounced; he walked more slowly. It irritated Susie no end to hear him pronounce his words like a recent immigrant from the Golden Horn.

One day an invitation to call for an interview came from a small company that specialized in mailing lists. Not yet completely automated, the firm was seeking mature people to—yes—stuff envelopes.

Jerry refused to consider going for the interview even though a letter had gone out over his signature soliciting it. Work like that was boring, he declared.

Boring! Victor exploded into a tirade about the poverty his family had endured and how his mother had had to take in laundry. No work was too demeaning as long as it was honest. In his own youth he had been asked to do some pretty lowdown things, including chaperoning his boss's mistress when she went shopping for lingerie.

For once Jerry asserted himself. "I'd sooner starve," he said in his best Laurence Olivier voice.

No danger of that, Susie thought, Public Opinion would see to it.

"I'll make the call," Victor offered. "I'll pay you just to go for the interview. You don't have to take the job."

But Jerry was adamant and nothing more was said. In fact, the entire subject of job hunting seemed to have been dropped altogether. Susie actually believed Victor had given up.

A couple of weeks later when Susie came to visit her father, he seemed unusually cheerful. He had something to show her, he said, and proudly displayed his latest acquisitions: a T-shirt with the motto, "I'm on the Team," and a plastic ID card with his smiling face under the heading, Employee Photo. The mailing list firm had hired him on the spot.

There was no more impersonating; Victor was too busy to be two people at once. He held the job until his death five years later.

With a modest inheritance from his dad, Jerry hung on. Just when he had almost depleted his resources, he met a location scout for a new television series who thought Jerry's apartment would make a perfect set. Jerry was paid thousands of dollars for the use of his apartment three or four times a year for *Precinct Alert*, which turned out to be one of the longest-running shows on TV. He even managed to play a bit part in one episode as a tyrannical father.

Goodbye, Evil Eye

It is not common knowledge that a woman sailed with Christopher Columbus. There are references to her in the peculiar melange of languages Columbus sometimes used in his diaries. This from a marginal note in his second Viaje: "*Et mulia tiene moltos sognos* [cares or dreams?] *sed mare* [or *madre*—ms. unclear] *non fecit.*" Perhaps she was of noble family, in hiding because of her religion (Jewish) or her pregnancy or both.

In the manner of Anastasia, women have come forward over the centuries, claiming to be descended from Columbus and his mysterious companion. With the exception of one Eli Matarasso, formerly of Izmir, Turkey, and later of Astoria, Queens, no other male has made this claim.

Flora Maimon had been born a Bar-David in Alexandria, Egypt. The official on Ellis Island, hearing the name Bar-David, wrote it as Bar *Doved* (having heard a little Yiddish in his time). The French word for dove is *colombe*, and one can only conjecture that Flora, a woman of great beauty and culinary prowess, did not fail to note the singular coincidence between the bird and the explorer. She had been primed by Arab fortune-tellers to believe that she was a princess and would cross the sea, as she had in another life, accompanied by an admiral. She had indeed crossed the sea, accompanied by a porcelain salesman, her husband Salvo Maimon. Perhaps while correcting the spelling of her maiden name, Flora showed the harried official the tiny cruciform scar in the crook of her left elbow, a small disfiguration with calligraphic indentations at each of the four extremities (north, south, east, etc.)

Her daughter Louise also bore this mark and assumed that, like buck teeth, it was a hereditary flaw. Flora had not revealed the scar's probable significance, this being one of the many mysteries Sephardic young women were expected to unravel through their own efforts.

Louise Maimon grew up surrounded by innuendo, learning to translate almost before she could speak. Her mother's invitation to a guest to loosen his necktie could be translated as: "Louise, open the window, I am dying of the heat." If Salvo said to Louise, "Correct me if I'm wrong," it meant that any disagreement between father and daughter would seriously undermine the very foundation of Jewish life and might well be the leading cause of heart attacks in Nassau County.

All of Louise's childhood illnesses were attended by the evil eye ritual administered by her mother. Who can say that it was not effective? Chicken pox and measles had left no trace on that olive-skinned, slightly surly countenance. Sitting at her daughter's bedside and clutching an ounce of salt in her right hand, Flora would recite her incantation, a mixture of begats and blessings, partly in Hebrew and partly in Ladino, the ancestral language still spoken in the Maimon home. If the spell was working, Flora found herself yawning uncontrollably. While Louise mimicked and giggled, Flora would continue to wave her hand over her daughter's head, never missing a word and smiling occasionally through her yawns. The incantation over, Louise was forced to endure the application of a little salt to her palate while the rest was thrown away over her left shoulder.

Once, during her freshman year, Louise made the mistake of enacting the ritual for the amusement of her friends in the NYU cafeteria. She poured a handful of salt from the greasy salt cellar and proceeded to wave her hand about, reciting whatever she could recall. To her astonishment she found herself yawning violently. Spilling the salt all over her advanced calculus book, she vowed never again to attempt the demonstration.

At thirty, Louise knew her family considered her a failure: no husband nor any prospects of one, and no hobbies. Recently she had dropped out of graduate school, the only woman in a doctoral program in mathematics, and was working intermittently for a public opinion firm.

One evening, while amusing herself with square roots and round numbers, she received an excited call from her father. He was phoning from Long Beach, Long Island, where her parents had a modest summer home. Her cousin Eliot would be arriving from California for a short visit the following Friday, and her father wanted Louise to come out to the house so she could drive them all to the airport to pick him up. Eliot had said he was coming "on urgent family business."

"Is it Eliot or his brother who's in genetic engineering?" she asked. "You know, cloning hardboiled eggs with our tax money?"

"This is America," her father said angrily. "People have opportunities here. You never had to walk barefoot to school like I did."

"Calm down, Dad. I'll be there."

Having met Eliot and his older brother Steve when they were all children, Louise was moderately curious about her relatives in California, of whom there were many. She visualized the two branches of the Maimon family on opposite coasts, keeping an entire continent in check between them. Her aunt Helen, Eliot and Steve's mother, was purportedly unstable because of her Lithuanian ancestry. According to family lore, she had led a "fast life" before her marriage. She and Salvo's brother Marco had eloped and, soon after, she gave birth "prematurely" to Steve. Aside from enjoying vacations without her husband, sign enough of mental illness, Helen's personality lacked what the Sephardim called *pimienta*, or pepper. She wore harlequin-shaped eyeglasses and continued to hope, after more than thirty years, that working with Chicano ladies would endear her to the Maimon family.

To Louise's father, California signified madness and blood. People who barbecued all day and drove 100 miles per hour on their freeways and who buried their pets with benefit of clergy were bound to be mad. Blood, on the other hand, meant family, and family was holiness. To Salvo, the shortest distance between New York and California was the number of relatives one could count on for accommodations. Blood was not always a guarantee of amity, however. During his brother Marco's last visit, the two men had nearly assaulted each other over the privilege of picking up the check at the International House of Pancake. Each had flung upon the table an awesome wad of bills; Salvo's face turned purple, his veins stood out, a veritable Noh mask of rage. Each brother had cursed the other in his zeal to convey the depth of his familial passion, but the proprietor intervened and the check was split.

How long was her cousin staying, Louise asked as she drove to the airport on Friday.

"These people don't tell you anything," Flora said.

"It's not nice to ask," Salvo said. "We can't chase him out of the house."

"Perhaps he would prefer a hotel," Louise suggested, thinking of the cramped house by the sea.

"Out of the question," her father said crisply. "It's not proper." Or, What would they say in California if we let him stay in a hotel? "Too bad my brother couldn't come too."

"Thank God," Flora said, sotto voce. "Marco would drive your father crazy. Californians have a different mentality."

At the airport, Salvo ran from one computer screen to another looking for information on the arrival of the flight. "Nobody gives you the right time of day," he fumed after failing to locate what he was looking for. "I always knew Pan Am was a lousy airline."

"But you said it was TWA," Louise said, checking the screen again. She dragged her parents off to the gate where passengers were just being discharged.

"Steve! Steve!" Salvo waved a frantic all-clear signal to a young man who had just emerged.

"*Steve?*" Louise said. "Eliot's brother? You told me Eliot was coming. Didn't Dad say Eliot was coming?"

"How can Eliot come?" her father called over his shoulder while pushing his way forward. "He's doing work for the government."

Steve—what was it Louise had been told about him, years ago? That he was a "drifter," because with a masters in sociology he had become a vegetarian, a day-care teacher, then a salesman for massage equipment. She had no idea what he was doing now. She knew that he had once been picked up for vagrancy because he was taking a walk on the road at night near his home. In California, it was understood that unless you had a dog, you did not walk.

Louise's first impression of her cousin was one of restrained ferocity. Perhaps it was his complexion, so unevenly dark that she could imagine him stubbornly sitting outdoors in the Sierras and letting the winds lash at him. No resemblance to anyone in the family, she decided. Good-looking for a cousin.

"You won't believe this," Louise said, maneuvering the car out of the lot, "but I was told your brother was coming."

"Eliot? He's busy making germs for the Pentagon."

Salvo slapped his nephew on the back. "What a sense of humor, just like your old man. No left turn here."

Seeing the sign pointing away from the city, Steve said he had made a hotel reservation.

"We'll cancel it," Salvo said.

"Besides, I bet you haven't had good Sephardic food in years," Flora said.

The party line, Louise thought. "How long are you staying?" She figured she would be doing her parents a favor by asking. "There's a lot to see."

"I'm just here for the weekend. I came for a particular reason. I want to see our grandfather's grave."

"There's a good show at the Music Hall," Salvo said.

"Poor kid," Flora murmured to her husband. "Lithuanians are morbid people."

"I hear you are in the appliance business," Salvo said.

"I used to sell massage equipment for motels. But that was a long time ago. Before I went into medicine." He explained that he was interning at a local hospital near L.A. It was rare for him to have an entire weekend off, but this was important. "I really want to visit your father's grave, Uncle Salvo."

"It's nice to be respectful," Salvo said uneasily as they turned into Oceanside Road.

The house in Long Beach was a far cry from the ancestral home by the Mediterranean, this bungalow facing a bike shop on the boardwalk and a frozen custard stand. No terraced hills or Moorish villas here, just green and pink stucco, split Georgian or nouveau saltbox houses, lawns decorated with reindeer or whitewashed jockeys holding lanterns, and a stretch of formerly genteel hotels now given over to the elderly and the deranged. It was not unusual to see a crone wandering up and down Beech Street in the middle of the night calling for her insurance agent. The great attraction was the sea air which, as everyone knew, cured all maladies. "I hope everyone is breathing," Flora said as she supervised installation on the porch.

"We'd be dead if we weren't," Louise said.

"But we have an eminent doctor with us," Salvo said, jovially, pointing to his nephew.

"Just an intern at North Hollywood General," Steve said. "Now about Grandpa . . ."

Seeing everyone inhaling satisfactorily, Flora retired to the kitchen. Aside from the ocean and the air, Long Beach was a wilderness for her. No friends, no music, no theater. Only dullards dropping in. Of course, she was always prepared. Four pounds of *borekas* happened to be ready at this very moment as well as two trays of *kadaif*, just in case. Certain people she could count on. Leon Habib was sure to make his appearance just at dinnertime. Naturally, she would ask him to stay.

Flora sighed. What happened to those promises made by the Arab fortune-tellers of her youth? What good had it done her to be descended from Christopher Columbus? She was lucky if Salvo condescended to take her out in a fishing boat.

On the porch, Steve was attempting to elicit some information about his grandfather. His father Marco had told him so little, he explained. Mostly along the lines of "Grandpa told us never to be fresh to our parents." Marco always added, "Wisdom worth a million bucks," before switching to the latest gossip about who was seen with whom at El Morocco.

"My father may he rest in peace was very wise, no question about it." Salvo tapped his fingers on the table. This boy's curiosity was unhealthy. What did he want to go poking around a grave for, especially one shrouded in bitterness. They had enough bodies in medical school. "How about the Boston Pops in Jones Beach? They are doing a tribute to Régine Crespin."

Louise rolled her eyes. Her father's musical taste

stopped with John Philip Sousa, an Ur-American whose music made his chest swell with pride. But in a house where a taste for classical music was usually deemed a sign of a daughter's snobbery, Régine Crespin took the honors. The famous singer was Sephardic—"*de los muestros,*" one of our people—and was no doubt related to Salvo's childhood friend from Turkey, Alberto Crespin, otherwise known as "*peppino,*" or cucumber.

"Dad, Louise said firmly, "Steve wants to see Grandpa's grave."

"A few *borekas?*" Flora appeared with a tray.

"It's far," Salvo said. "Hard to get to. It's in Brooklyn."

"I thought it was in Queens," his daughter said.

"Queens, Brooklyn, it's a big place."

"The sun is so hot." Flora fanned herself. "I don't care, but Louise thought we should have an awning."

"Oh yes," Louise said almost automatically. "I'm just dying to have a blue scalloped awning here."

"Her father can't refuse her anything," Flora said fondly.

"Next year, God willing, we'll fix up this place."

"God has nothing to do with it," Louise said. "Macy's has them on sale."

"Is there some secret about where he's buried?" Steve asked. "Can't you just tell me?"

But Louise's parents had risen just then to greet a neighbor on the adjoining balcony.

"They can't tell you much because they don't know," Louise said, taking a perverse delight in Steve's persistence. "Or rather, there are different versions of everything. For instance, my dad will say that he was born in 1927, then another time it will be 1928. Some days the name of the cemetery is Cedars of Lebanon, other times it's Cypress Hills."

Steve looked uncomfortably at his aunt and uncle who had resumed their seats. Salvo was smiling and nodding, Flora was surreptitiously loosening her brassiere to facilitate respiration.

"I paid my respects last month," Salvo said, "but Leon was driving so I didn't pay attention."

"So we should call this Leon," Steve prompted.

"No need," his cousin said. "He is number one moocher and should be turning the corner in exactly five seconds."

"He's an old friend," Salvo said.

"Louise is right," his wife said. "Now we'll be stuck with him all evening." She leaned over the railing. "Yoo-oo, Leon . . ."

Leon Habib: old schoolfellow of Salvo's from Turkey, former U.S. Army major, and present-day miser. He likes to drop in for lunch at the Nahums, for dinner at the Maimons, for coffee at the Bensignors. Everyone vies for his company: Flora because of her reputation as cook; the Soninos because, known as "the Vatican," they feel an obligation to those less fortunate; the Hamaouis because they cheated Leon's family two centuries earlier in Iraq. Everyone complains of his stinginess, the lack of reciprocity (not that they would want to go to his apartment, moldy with bachelor life). Occasionally he brings a miniscule box of chocolate kisses, such as the one he now presents to Flora while welcoming Steve to the bosom ("if I may be so bold") of the family.

"Leon is taking us out to dinner," Salvo announces.

"With pleasure," answers Leon, roaring with laughter.

Salvo says, "You can't take it with you."

"But he can try," says Louise.

"Now, now, young lady . . ." Leon wags his finger. "I knew you when you had a bare bottom. What happened to that boyfriend of yours, the Russian fellow?"

"He got me pregnant and I had an abortion. Then he decided he was gay."

"*Mon dieu*," Leon blushes. "*Quelle histoire.*"

"She's teasing," Flora says. "Have some salad."

Steve's eyes meet Louise's. She blushes. Didn't one of the Ptolemys marry his sister? Cousins were a much healthier combination.

"Your uncle tells me you are in the appliance business."

"*Es medico*," Salvo says in Ladino as though he were revealing shameful information.

"How come I'm the first doctor in the family? After all, Maimonides was the great healer and our name is Maimon."

"We can't stand the sight of blood," Louise said.

"The name is just a coincidence," Salvo said. "Besides, Maimonides was a radical."

"We are registered Democrats," Flora said, offering round yet another tray of food.

"About that grave . . ."

"Ah yes," Leon said, "if I recall correctly, it is near a fence." Leon was the treasurer of the burial society and spoke with some authority. The society had been formed for the sole purpose of burying its members who, in the meantime, held frequent picnics and boat-rides.

"Just follow the highway," Salvo said. "Cypresses of Lebanon. It's closed on Saturdays."

"I'll go on Sunday then. I'll change my flight to a later one."

"Can't you go another time, dear?" Flora asked. "The beach will be so lovely this weekend, according to the weather reports." How would it look, writing to the relatives: *We showed him the sights and then took him to the cemetery?*

"I can't give you the precise location since I am only the treasurer of the society and our records keeper is recovering from his prostate. However, when you get there—it's Cedars of Lebanon—they will tell you." Leon looked at his watch and abandoned his seat with regret. He was due at the next house for dessert.

"What's your hurry?" asked Salvo. "The night is young. You don't mind taking down the garbage, do you?"

It was too early for bed, so the two young people went for a stroll on the boardwalk. Louise wondered if he was seeing anyone. What a pity they were related. "You seem pretty well-balanced for someone from California," she said.

"But you're wondering why I want to spend time at a grave instead of going to hear some jazz with a beautiful cousin, right? I'll tell you why."

When he was pre-med, an angel had appeared to him in a dream and confirmed what he had always suspected: The Maimons were indeed descended from Moses Maimonides, the great physician. In the dream the angel held the caduceus in one hand—that winged staff with the two snakes coiled around it, the symbol of the medical profession—and in the other hand, a jar of yogurt. (Yes, Louise remembered, the pioneer who had brought yogurt to America had been *de los muestros*.) The angel had commanded Steve to found a clinic based on Maimonides' teachings.

"But how did the angel know you were pre-med?" she asked—then caught herself. "Of course, there was no pre-med in Maimonides' time," she added. But they did have mathematics. She thought with sudden nostalgia of infinite and irrational numbers, the glimpses she'd had into charmed quarks and astrophysics.

Louise looked up at the stars. "The Ptolemaic system," she murmured. "Earth as the center of the universe. Ptolemy was also from Alexandria, like my mom." Dreamily she rubbed the scar on her elbow. Steve looked at her. He seemed to understand.

With rain threatening on Saturday morning, Flora suggested that the young people drive to Coney Island to visit their grandmother at the Sephardic senior citizens home, thereby permitting her and Salvo to skip their biweekly visit. The idea was greeted with enthusiasm by Steve who thought that perhaps Nona might know where her husband's grave was.

"She doesn't even know her own son," Flora said, draining her cup of Turkish coffee and peering into the grounds. "My goodness, what do I see?"

"I don't know," Louise said rhetorically, "what do you see?"

"I don't see the sugar," Salvo said, waving his spoon.

"Louise is going to be very lucky." Flora studied the dregs.

"That's what you told me last time, Mom."

"What nonsense," Salvo said. "You call yourselves liberated women? Isn't there any sugar in this house?"

"Louise is going on a trip," Flora said.

"I stopped tripping in high school."

"Make fun," her mother said, "I don't mind."

"Remind me to show you my blue stone," Louise said. "It's supposed to keep the evil eye away from me."

"It seems to be working so far," Steve said.

"Bravo," his aunt said. "I'm glad you understand."

"I just remembered," Louise said. "There's a fortune-teller in town. A friend of mine went to her recently. She might be able to locate a grave."

Salvo laughed. "I don't think they work on Saturdays. They probably have a union. Goddam unions." He frowned.

Flora was putting together a parcel for Salvo's mother, the candies Leon had brought and a woolen sweater. Nona would probably complain about the color. "Last time she wanted blue," Flora said, "I brought her blue. Then she said she preferred brown. Tell her this is brown." It was purple.

"You know she can't eat those candies, *chérie*."

"They can't go empty-handed. I don't want to hear that her children neglect her. Let her give the candy to the nurses." The old woman would probably cram everything underneath her mattress.

The veranda of the Coney Island Sephardic Senior Home was lined with aluminum chairs where the elderly sat on warm days, looking out at the ocean. For the visitor, entering was like running the gauntlet. Arms reached out to touch, canes waved imperiously, intimate questions were asked. "Do you have a husband?" "Is your belly fruitful?" And now to Louise, "Are you Shemaria's granddaughter?" Pointing to Steve, "Is he one of us?" (Not, Is he gentile? but, Is he Sephardic or one of the others, an Ashkenazi?) Followed by Steve, Louise went down the receiving line, smiling (how her parents would have been surprised). "Be healthy," she said in Ladino. "May you live a long time." Hands tugged at her. "I knew your grandfather," a fierce looking man said and Steve gasped with joy. His Ladino was rudimentary but serviceable.

Nona's room faced the sea and the "Cyclone" roller coaster. She was eighty-eight and illiterate. Great tufts of white hair protruded from her ears like antennae. Without turning at their entrance she said in Ladino,

"Are you Salvo's wife?"

Louise went around and faced her grandmother.

"Look, Nona, I'm your granddaughter and this is your grandson Steve."

"My grandsons never come to see me. Where is Salvo?"

"He couldn't come, he had work to do," Louise lied.

"You shouldn't work on the Sabbath," Nona said and began to rock in her chair. Steve had taken her hand but she seemed not to notice. She stopped rocking and said, "They told me he wouldn't come. Bring me a thimble next time."

Louise slowly explained who Steve was.

"His mother is that Lithuanian woman." Nona lapsed into vehement Armenian, perhaps cursing.

A staff worker came in with a tray. "Come on honey, here's your lunch."

"This one stole my package," Nona said.

"She saying I stole her package again? Is this it, sweetie?" She produced a paper bag from a drawer.

"I don't want it. Tell her to throw it away."

"She'll want it later. I'll just set it down here on the shelf." The woman went out.

Nona poured her coffee into her soup. "They left me

here to die," she said with satisfaction. "Where is the sweater?" But before Louise could open the parcel she said, "Hide it or they'll steal it. Under the mattress, quick!"

Steve jumped up and did as she asked.

"Why didn't they let me dance at your wedding?" she asked. "I can't walk but I can dance."

Downstairs someone was playing a Greek song on the piano and people were stamping in rhythm.

"Nona," Steve said, "tell me about your husband." He spoke slowly, unsure of his Ladino.

"The wife must obey the husband," Nona said. "It's the law." Suddenly she began to cry. "He was the light of my life. The boys quarreled." Tears were streaming down her face. "I couldn't do anything."

Louise put her arm around her. "We're here now. See, this is Steve. He came from far away."

Nona smiled through her tears. "I knew he would come. It says so in the holy book." She turned toward the window. The roller coaster was descending. She began to rock again. It was clear that there was no point in asking her where her husband was buried.

"Let's go to your fortune-teller," Steve said when they got back to the car.

"You? A man of science?"

"Whatever works." There was a slightly mad glint in his eye. The ocean was shimmering like plastic, and shots could be heard from the penny arcade.

Reverend B. Jonas practiced her ministry at the Church of All Souls on the second floor above the Eclair Konditorei where fortunate members of Central Europe went for *Kaffee und Kuchen*.

A large middle-aged woman ushered them into a small chapel whose walls were covered with wallpaper resembling stained glass. She led them to the back and sat down at a desk facing them. Several drawing pens were hooked neatly into her jacket pocket as though messages from different regions of the underworld were conveyed in specific colors. There was nothing on the desk except a clock and a container of coffee.

"Twenty-five dollars in advance," she said. "Cash or any major credit card. Try and deduct it from your major medical. You come here because your soul is ailing."

After handing over the money, Steve said he wanted to locate a grave since no one seemed to know where it was.

Dr. Jonas closed her eyes. A cat moved across the floor and sat at Louise's feet. She shifted nervously.

"I see an elderly lady in a polyester suit carrying an umbrella. Not a relative, a teacher maybe . . . someone who has passed on."

"I don't know any old teachers," Steve said dubiously.

"I tell it as it is given," the Reverend said sharply, eyes still closed. "There is an old man with a goatee. . . . He greets you."

"Grandpa," Louise breathed.

"He is happy. He has a flower in his buttonhole, a pink—" Suddenly she sneezed. "Excuse me, I'm allergic to roses." She opened her eyes, which were watering, and blew her nose. Resuming, "He is—uhmm—singing." She began a low hum that sounded like "Swing Low, Sweet Chariot." The cat put one paw up on Louise's chair. She shrank back.

"Wait," Dr. Jonas said. "This man, he did not go to his rest in peace. Oh no no. These people at the grave, they are arguing. The priest—"

"Rabbi," Louise said.

"In the spirit world all are ministers of the Lord and if you want a cheap job you all can go next door to the gypsy lady. I tell it as it is given to me. By the way, don't leave your camera in the car."

"Too late," Steve said.

"I see—a hospital. Old man writing. He's got a little black box, shining. A shining . . . it's not clear. Wait— it's in the eyes—it *is* the eyes. Someone else has his eyes. Is it you, darling?"

"Giving his eyes to science!" Steve whispered. "It all ties in."

"Oh my, oh my. The old man's sons, they are having some fracas. He wants to tell me something. I see a wall. A stone, a stone near a tower."

Steve gripped Louise's hand.

"In the sea there's a tower, in the tower there's a window. . . . At the window she calls to sailors. Oh, why are you seasick, dear?"

Louise swallowed. The ground seemed to be tilting. Salt was on her tongue. "That's from a song," she told Steve. "Nona used to sing it." To Reverend Jonas, "How come you're giving the words in English?"

"In the world of the soul, all languages are one."

Louise took a deep breath.

"Take it easy," Steve said, holding her hand.

"It passes," Reverend Jonas said. "All journeys end. There's that desert again."

"What desert?" Louise asked faintly.

"California," Steve said.

"It's the land of the fair . . . the old man has gone to the land of the fair—Pharaoh."

"Maimonides," Steve said quietly.

Of course. The great teacher had gone into exile in Egypt. Even Louise knew that. Knew the story about the emperor Saladin who had called on Maimonides to attend his captive, Richard the Lion-Hearted. This was one of the few highlights of eight stultifying years of Hebrew school.

Dr. Jonas opened her eyes. "If you want more, it's an-other twenty-five dollars. I charge by the hour. Maybe you all would like to know which stocks are going up?" Her fingers played temptingly with her pens, but the two cousins were already at the door.

Saturday morning services at the Sephardic synagogue in Long Beach were extremely refined, as befitted the descendants of grandees. To go to the Ashkenazi temple would have been unthinkable. Flora shuddered at their pronunciation and the unseemly emotion of the rabbi, who sobbed while praying.

She settled back in her balcony seat and looked around critically. There was Mrs. Camhi with her green eyeshadow and plain daughter. What a pity Louise refused to join the young adult group here.

The new rabbi walked slowly to the pulpit and folded his hands. Perhaps they were shaking. He was trying hard, one had to say that for him. Always apologizing for being born an Ashkenazi (the congregation had had to take him for lack of qualified Sephardic candidates). But to give him credit, he had recently written an article about Chief Justice Benjamin Cardozo who was *de los muestros*.

"Today," he began, "I should like to speak about the personal habits of the Jew at war. . . ." Flora's mind ran back to her oven: one spinach, one tomato, one leek pie. Enough for a dozen unexpected guests.

". . . The soldier must maintain the highest moral and hygienic standards. The law prescribes that the soldier shall have a place outside the camp wherein he shall attend to his bodily functions. With his gear he shall have a shovel . . ."

What a soothing voice he had. If only he were ten years younger and unmarried.

". . . The personal habits of the soldier of Israel are part of his artillery." Flora unbuttoned the top button of her blouse. She was feeling warm. Politics did not belong in the synagogue.

The rabbi raised his arms impressively."Contagion can mean disaster." My God, was he talking about venereal disease? Why had Louise broken off with her last boyfriend? "He contaminated me," was all she would volunteer; then she went off to Philadelphia and returned almost emaciated, a fearful reminder of how she had been at sixteen. Anorexia, Louise had called it, a lovely name like that of a Greek goddess, but the ultimate cruelty to a mother.

Down below in the men's section, Salvo was think-ing that this rabbi had no style. Speaking about war like a milquetoast. Louise couldn't abide the poor rabbi. But she had strange ideas, expecting a clergy-man to be out protesting and sleeping with the home-less. An odd child, his daughter. He remembered her studying "probability" and arguing with him. Salvo laughing and wondering what there was to study. Probability meant that something might happen or it might not. Marriage would shape her up. And never mind love. His brother Marco had been in love and see where that had gotten him.

Love, to Salvo, denoted illicit relationships such as those between business executives and their mistresses. Husbands and wives, in Salvo's vocabulary, should like each other and get along. Marco was so besotted with his wife that for each of her birthdays he had built an addition to their house in Santa Monica. Salvo had seen with his own eyes the wishing well, the sauna, the orchids in the greenhouse, and God knows what.

How misguided this boy was to look for the old man's grave.

Only Salvo's vigilance had prevented disaster when his revered father died. No one had taken the elder Maimon seriously when he announced on his deathbed that he wished to give his body to science, stating it in his will, with a separate clause for the eyes. Never, said Salvo, it was against holy law. The old man, so orthodox, had become unhinged. Marco had been willing to bargain. "Maybe not the whole body, but just the eyes? It's his last wish." But Salvo had been adamant; if not for him, their father would not now be lying peacefully between two shopping centers in Long Island—or Queens—but would have been chopped in pieces for "science." Science was good, it was important, even the rabbi was talking about it now: technology in war, shovels, trenches . . . But there had to be a limit.

The service over, Salvo folded up his prayer shawl and went to find his wife with whom he got along so well.

The cousins found a restaurant overlooking the water where they could gorge themselves on shellfish, forbidden food to be consumed, always, with a slight frisson of guilt.

"Another reason for coming east is that I wanted to get a feel for the family," Steve said.

"The great myth of family," Louise grimaced. What was it like growing up in California?" she asked.

Steve's mother hated California, she learned. His parents quarreled constantly, shouting at each other from opposite ends of the family room where the furniture was arranged for maximum lack of communication. One time when he was very young, his father said something so dreadful to his mother that she clapped her hands over the boy's ears. "I heard it anyway, but I can't remember it. All I remember is that she said he didn't mean it, that he really loved me. As though what he said was some kind of attack on me. That part of it stuck in my mind."

He seemed to be turning morose. To divert him, Louise asked what he was planning to specialize in.

"Family medicine," he said, which struck them both as absurd.

The Cedars of Lebanon straddled the no-man's-land between Queens and Brooklyn, with the Expressway dividing the waves of headstones. It was early Sunday morning. Steve looked pale. "There's something wrong," he said. "I can feel it."

"You're right. It's not open yet. I could have slept another hour." Louise was beginning to tire of his obsession.

"Here's this angel," Steve said slowly. Was he talking to her or to himself? "There's a staff in the angel's hand. He tells me to found a clinic. He's holding a jar of yogurt. That's the part I don't understand."

"Maybe you should start a health food restaurant instead."

At that moment the gates swung open, probably activated by remote control.

The place was immense. Every trade, every lodge had its resting place. Knights of Pythias, Elks, Moose, Friends of Wildlife (how did they get in here?), Oddfellows . . . They continued walking, past the United Jewish Printers, Amalgamated Tailors, Furriers, Leatherworkers, the Association of Jews from Sofia, Monastir, Salonika, Rhodes, Izmir. And then they stopped in front of a black gate with a sign. Home ground for the Sephardic Burial Society.

A tremor went through the young man. "Hey," Louise said and touched his shoulder. Steve's teeth were chattering. She drew him to a nearby bench and made him sit down.

Directly facing the bench was a headstone with a miniature oval photograph propped against it, a young woman in a high-necked dress. The inscription on the stone said, in Ladino, "You are gone but we remember you, Sarina." Sarina had been born on the isle of Corfu. Perhaps she had crossed the Atlantic in a rickety boat, eating nothing but olives and biscuits.

"You know, I realized very early in my life that my dad preferred my brother Eliot," Steve said. "He still hasn't forgiven me for turning down his graduation present, a paid night with a whore. He laughed when I said it was undignified for a descendant of Maimonides. Then he said, 'It's okay, I love you just the same,' and I was reminded of that time I told you about, when he said something my mother didn't want me to hear, years back." Steve shook his head and stood up. "I've tried to remember what it was so many times, but it just escapes me."

They picked their way through paths overgrown with perpetual care and found the grave at last, topped by a nondescript slab, etched with the name in Hebrew and English, date of birth and death. Nothing more. Steve closed his eyes. Louise moved away, leaving him free for whatever revelation might be forthcoming.

After a moment he opened his eyes wide, his mouth twisted. "I remember," he shouted and staggered toward her. "I remember what he said to her. He said, 'You and your brat.' Not his brat. *Somebody else's.*" His voice was hoarse. *"My father was—somebody else— a stranger."*

Soon after Steve's return to Los Angeles, Salvo received an irate letter from his brother Marco, saying that he'd been compelled to tell Steve the truth about his parentage. Besides Helen, of course, Salvo was the only other person who knew the secret. Not even Flora knew.

Marco was not Steve's father. Before he married Helen she had had an affair and gotten pregnant; the father had disappeared. Marco had married her anyway, despite his brother's disapproval.

Marco also had to tell Steve about (may he rest in peace) the old man's thwarted desire to donate his organs to science and accused Salvo of aiding and abetting the boy in his ridiculous search for the grave.

Salvo was furious. So much for the Maimon family motto ("Peace at any price"). Had Marco taken Salvo's advice years ago, he would not have fallen in love and would not have had to bring up another man's son.

The information was given to Louise at the tail end of a phone conversation with her mother about Xavier Cugat, the Latin bandleader known as the king of the conga, rhumba, cha-cha, etc. and his ascension to the ranks of *los muestros*, courtesy of the Sephardic community of Long Beach.

The news about Steve was like the discovery of a new solar system.

Give him time, Louise said to herself. He'll call when he's ready. In the meantime, after several recurring dreams about parabolas and vectors, she decided to return to graduate school. Some dreams were reliable.

"This is your former cousin," Steve said when he finally phoned after a month. "I've learned that angels make mistakes too. Even your fortune-teller was taken in." He had started a search for his real father. Also, he was switching from family medicine to psychiatry, a profession unrecognized in the Sephardic enclaves of New York, Los Angeles, and possibly Seattle.

"And what about you?" he inquired. Might she come

out for a visit—to relatives?

Something lurched inside her. "Stay tuned for lift-off," she said. It became suddenly clear to Louise that if Steve could investigate the inner workings of the mind, she could explore the outer reaches of the universe, either as an astronaut or, more likely, as a cartographer of outer space. In the meantime there were earthly delights to contemplate, since Steve had promised to stay in touch.

When after a year it became clear that Louise was flying out to the West Coast more often than was healthy, and no other man was spoken about save her thesis advisor, Flora began to allow herself to plan. Surely the union between a California doctor and the putative descendant of Christopher Columbus would merit being recorded in History rather than in the *Long Island Daily Press*.

And it came to pass in one of those wedding palaces off the Sunrise Highway that the rabbi proclaimed in suburban Hebrew the authenticity of the marriage contract drawn up several thousand years ago in the original Aramaic (holding it up for viewing) and now validated in Roslyn Heights. But once the bandleader had ordered all those couples who married for sex, for love, for money, out on the floor, and when he had done with asking for applause for the happy couple (a quick glance at his notes for the names), then blood took over, the blood of the Sephardim. It fired up the instrumentalists, and cowed the rabbi and the small

Ashkenazi contingent on the groom's mother's side, and music erupted. The women threw back their heads, and shimmied, while the men, aged but smoldering, stamped their feet provocatively. The Greek guests did their decorous ceremonial dance. There was even a belly dancer, Marco's present, quivering her body as men stuffed dollar bills into her sequined bosom.

Louise's mother insisted that her daughter wear around her neck the hand-shaped talisman, the *hamsa*, she had received from her own mother before coming to America. Within the amulet was a piece of parchment with faded Hebrew lettering. The words, however, would not be Hebrew but Ladino: "*El Almirante estaba enamorado de* . . . [blurred] *mujer, hija de David.*" The admiral loved . . . [?] woman, daughter of David.

Like the compass-shaped scar on Louise's elbow, this was another link to the illustrious explorer, which she would have to discover on her own.

Arbitration

"Put another pillow there. Another one." My father points imperiously at the armchair where he is about to be installed, an oriental potentate. Like the princess and the pea, he needs more and more padding.

Groaning, he settles into his throne. "Ayyy . . . they're all thieves," he mutters. He means the world at large, anyone outside his immediate circle except for Franklin Delano Roosevelt.

Though he is feeble, he still relishes the role he is to play today, that of arbitrator. There is nothing that pains him more than to see members of a family at war, nothing he likes so well as to bring the opposing factions together. Today's case involves Dave Cicourel, also known as the Mayor of Casablanca. Dave is eighty like my father, whom he has known since their school days in Izmir, Turkey. Dave's second wife has left him after three months of marriage and he wants her back.

"The wife belongs with the husband" is one of my father's tenets, along with "Brothers' quarrels are always mended" and "Every girl should receive secretarial training."

In despair over the dereliction of his wife, Dave Cicourel wanders through his cluttered apartment, his senses dulled by *raki*, the anisette liquor, a sweet licorice of oblivion. The booty of half a century on the waterfront surrounds him. Unclaimed goods: silks, amphorae, brass sphinxes, jars of olives, pine nuts, grape leaves, fetid feta cheese, rancid almonds, halvah. Every hostess shudders at his approach for he never comes empty-handed. "How many green olives can a couple eat?" my mother asks and promptly throws out whatever he brings. Dave worked as a longshoreman, then as a supervisor on New York's waterfront. Incorruptible, he personally thrashed anyone caught stealing cargo. The mafia tried without success to buy him.

During World War II, Dave was a major in the U.S. Army and led the cleanup operations in Morocco. There were still pockets of German resistance when he set up his headquarters in Casablanca. Slowly the Jewish remnant crept out of hiding. It was Dave who provided them with food, shelter, and papers, cutting through the bureaucracy of many countries and sending countless survivors on to new lives and safety. Under an obscure Spanish law of 1924 that granted citizenship to all Sephardim, he was able to obtain numerous Spanish passports. Where civil rule had broken down, he became the final authority. For years after the war people would stop him on the streets of three continents to express their gratitude.

His voice was loud, his manners crude; he never announced himself before a visit. In his seventy-fifth year he carried a crate of sesame breads five flights up to a wedding luncheon.

This oaf of a man had been married for fifty-two years to the flower of Sephardic aristocracy, a regal woman who claimed descent from the Abravanels of Cordova. He treated her like a serf, a harem of one, according to my mother who has a vested interest in Sephardic sociology. But how he mourned her when she died, this Rachel la Hermosa. For months he did not leave his apartment. (The smell, God forbid, my father said. You wouldn't want to set foot.) He lay about unshaven amidst his spoils, dreaming of a new wife who would ply him with subservience and Turkish delight.

"He needs to be married," my father said at the time. "He is looking for a wife."

"Someone to cook for him," I said.

"No, you know—sex, everything," he said delicately.

My mother howled.

"He needs it," my father said stubbornly. Then under his breath, "I pity the poor woman."

Dave Cicourel's quest was pursued with as much zeal as any in mythology. No scholar, he nonetheless became

skilled in research techniques and was soon in contact
with ecclesiastical authorities in all parts of the globe,
for this new wife would come through unimpeachable
sources.

One of his early leads was to a widow in Laurel
Canyon, California. My uncle who lived in Los Angeles
was dispatched as a scout. She plied him with rose
water and sugar syrup and cried. So far so good. She
had of course heard of Dave Cicourel, as who hadn't
among our kinsmen.

Not matrimony but an old age home by the sea was
what she longed for. Dave went to California hoping
she would relent. She wept again. She did not have the
fare to get to New York, where it was necessary for her
to establish residency in order to become eligible for the
Sephardic Home for the Aged in Coney Island. Dave
brought her to New York, installed her chastely at a relative's, and then got her into the home of her dreams,
once more the benefactor.

Then there was a seamstress in Brooklyn, recom-
mended by a rabbi. Though she was willing, a techni-
cality prevented the marriage. Her husband had left her
years earlier, never to be seen again. According to
Jewish law she was still his wife until such time as he
requested a divorce. "I wanted her," Dave lamented.
"She was young."

"She was seventy, not counting Saturdays, Sundays,
and holidays," my father said later. "She was lucky to
escape. You don't know this man. You know how he

gets those sesame breads?"

"Smuggled in from Crotona Avenue?"

"You're close." Dave bought them from Abolafia in the Bronx, a man everyone fears. To buy the bread one must also buy the cheese or Abolafia will sic his dogs on you. The cheese is always rotten. Exempt from this rider, Dave is everyone's conduit for the bread.

My father picks up an empty glass. A lesson will follow. "If Dave Cicourel says to you, 'This is cardboard,' then this is cardboard."

After several months of widowerhood, this great stallion was reduced to barging in on sisterhood bazaars and offering himself as a raffle prize. In the end he met his second wife by a railing on Riverside Drive, where she was symbolically casting her sins to the waters on the first day of the New Year. And now, three months after the wedding, she had gone crying to the rabbi who married them, complaining of "mistreatment."

At Dave's request my father has agreed to use his good offices to reconcile them. He is often chosen for this function. Not because of his knowledge of juridical procedures, but because he believes in the inviolability of marriage and in the deleterious effects of family strife.

Dave arrives first, bearing tributes, my father's weight in chocolates and a bouquet of roses. My mother eyes the candies suspiciously. The boxes are dusty. She knows there is green fuzz around the pralines.

The conversation, like all crucial ones involving

these people, is circuitous.

"How are you?" Dave asks.

"Everything is in the hands of God," my father says.

They speak of the state of the world, the latest rent increase. My father begins a tirade against landlords. "It makes you understand why people get so mad they take a stick—a big stick—and go and attack the landlord. Believe me, if I wasn't so short . . ." They speak of the latest strikes: bus drivers, dock workers, Dave's old stomping ground. "I don't know," my father says, "there's no respect for law and order. People taking matters into their own hands. Anarchy, anarchy." Then he curses in Greek as the doorbell rings.

Victoria, the wife, top-heavy in the mink stole Dave gave her, fear in her eyes. Her rings slide up and down her thin fingers. "Ah, the bride," my mother says gaily and kisses her. Victoria avoids looking at Dave who is holding the bouquet like a torch.

"Everything is wonderful, wonderful," my father pronounces ex cathedra.

Victoria sniffles and pulls out her handkerchief.

"Why don't we have something to eat?" Mother's solution.

"The honey pastry that my mother of blessed memory used to make would turn to sour bile on my lips," Victoria says, speaking in Ladino. "He has taken vengeance on my soul. If I had the sky for paper, the sea for ink, a tree for my pen, I still could not describe all my misery."

"Fine, fine," my father says in English. "Let's not get

excited. *Chérie*, more coffee," he commands my mother. "So what's the problem? First of all, everything should be fifty-fifty. This is a democracy."

"Democracy?" my mother echoes dubiously. "In this house?"

"*Mi amor*," Dave says at last, his voice hoarse. "I just want the best for you."

"At my age," Victoria continues in Ladino, "a woman wants rest. Trees cry for rain and mountains for air, and that is how these eyes of mine are crying. It is terrible to be a stranger."

"But we are all strangers," Mother says. "I came here from Egypt, you came from Bulgaria, Dave from Izmir—"

"Let's get down to business," Dave says, still holding the roses stiffly, as though he expected a bee to fly out at him.

"First of all," my father says, "you should keep separate bank accounts. You never know."

"I never had my own bank account," my mother says. "You wouldn't let me."

"*Chérie*, please." My father raps his knuckles on the arm of his chair.

"I bought her a house," Dave says. "In Rockaway."

He hadn't asked her first and she didn't want it.

"Rockaway is beautiful," my father says. "By the sea. Just like Izmir."

"This is nothing," Mother says, a friend of the court. "The house can be sold."

With sudden inspiration my father says to Dave, "I hope you are not making—unreasonable demands. At your age . . ."

"What are you talking about?" Dave stuffs the flowers behind his cushion and lumbers over to the upright piano. "Can you do this?" He braces himself and lifts the leonine foot of the instrument several inches off the floor.

Mother shrieks and Father flails wildly on his perch.

Victoria reaches out a trembling hand. "For God's sake, David!" On her face is a look—is it?—of near admiration. He straightens up, panting.

"This is a *man*," my father says to one and all. "No wonder he was the Mayor of Casablanca."

"He certainly deserves another cup of coffee." Mother bustles around.

And Victoria has changed her seat. Now she is beside her husband who is still panting and mopping his forehead.

"*Los hombres son locos*," she says. Men are crazy. This is the first time she smiles. She is suddenly attractive. Her eyes shine darkly, there is a mole on her cheek. Unlike other women who age rapidly, Sephardic women seem to develop new layers of beauty like old paintings.

"I only want your happiness, *mi querida*," Dave says.

"You see," my father summing up fondly. "He means well. Only David, you have to be a little more gentle. Victoria is not a piano."

"Or a crate of sesame breads," Mother says and bursts into song: "My bride's door is open and she appears *como la primavera—*" like spring itself.

"Next case." My father rubs his hands.

The Voyager

I went to visit my father in the hospital. He had recently been taken out of Intensive Care. During his absence, my mother had cleaned out his drawers and given me his travel diary. "Here," she said, "I know you like to read," as though it were a vice never mentioned in company. Indeed, my father likes to say that too much reading can make a person crazy. Like syphilis, I suppose.

The diary was written in 1919 when my father was twenty years old. It is a record of his forty-five-day voyage to America from Izmir, Turkey, on board a Greek ship in third—not steerage—class.

At the hospital I found him politely abusing the West Indian nurse, careful to call her Dear while complaining about the service. "You are not the only patient, Mr. Touriel," she said, fluffing his pillow.

When she had left the room he said, without having

greeted me or otherwise acknowledging my existence, "We are completely at their mercy." He took a sip of fresh cold water. "Do you realize that these hospitals would not be able to run without all these foreigners? How is your husband?"

(Never how am I, his daughter.) I told him: The great white father my lord and master was well. As an afterthought he asked about the children.

I waved the diary at him. "I didn't know your French was so elegant. Do you recognize this?" I read him the passage in which he describes taking leave of his family in language worthy of Victor Hugo, though the spelling left a little to be desired.

He listened, enraptured. "I wrote it," he said, marveling. In another passage he invokes God frequently and swears to his father that he will never commit any *frivolités*. "I stuck to it," he said. "Read me some more."

"I'm trying to find a good section," I said. But the rest of the diary comprised almost nothing but descriptions of food. As I read snatches to him I became more and more exasperated. Today I ate three black olives because the lentils were dirty. At lunch they served us stringy beans. I ate no bread. Day after day, forty-five days, a young man crossing the Atlantic Ocean and all he can talk about is his diet.

At this point the nurse brought in his lunch tray. "The food is very good here," my father said, offering me some consommé. "I told Mother she should take home some of the menus so she can make the same things." My mother is the most extraordinary cook among all the Sephardim of Manhattan, Brooklyn, the Bronx, and Lawrence-Cedarhurst combined. She has had recipes printed in the *New York Times*.

"Ay," he grimaced as he shifted position and language. "Nobody gives a damn," he said in Ladino. "The doctors don't tell you anything. A dog is better off."

How often had I begged him to switch doctors. But he would not hear of it. Dr. Saporta had gone to the same Alliance Israélite school as my father back in the village in Turkey. He would have been insulted. I could see my father in perpetual thrall to his childhood buddy, following a code as rigid as that of a sinister fraternal order.

He shot out his finger and pointed to the window. "See that meat market?" he said in English. "There, on your right—follow me—on your *right*. That's how medicine is, a business."

I offered to call Dr. Saporta now, this minute, to suggest a consultation with another physician.

"But they don't cooperate," my father said plaintively. "They have ethics. They don't like it when you switch. He has a nasty nurse." I moved toward the phone, but he said, No, all right, he would call himself. He wanted to congratulate the doctor on his son's wedding anyway.

I had to dial the number for him, his fingers were shaking so.

"Fine, fine, Doctor," he said when he got through. *Doctor.* They were childhood friends with bloody knees and runny noses. "No complaints, no complaints. Everything is wonderful." His entire arm was trembling. I took the receiver and held it for him. The doctor had evidently switched to Ladino, so my father joyously congratulated him on his son's wedding, wishing him much *allegria*.

"Ask him," I whispered.

"Tell me, Doctor—I don't want to take up your time, I know you are a busy man . . ." A little trickle of saliva had formed at the corner of my father's mouth and began to dribble down his chin. I took the phone away.

"Doctor," I said, very businesslike, introducing myself using my married name, but the doctor said, "Ah yes, Lucy, I remember when you were in diapers." Nonetheless, I stated the case. He turned cool but equally businesslike. Yes, he would be glad to send on the X-rays.

"You see," I said to my father.

"Lousies, lousies," he said, turning his face away.

"Why do you stick with him?" I asked. My parents had done nothing but complain about this doctor for thirty years. They spoke of the dirt in his waiting room, the "horse pills," his brusque manner.

"We were more or less satisfied," my father said. Then he added bitterly, "These people give themselves airs. Some of them can't read and write and they are millionaires today. Peasants. They used to eat with their fingers."

"Look." I opened the diary to a place I had marked.

The ship in the adjacent berth is manned by a black Hindu crew. They make a little pile of food and then, bent over their plates, *they eat with their fingers.*

"They were very clean," he said seriously.

"But what else? Did you make any friends, did you see any astonishing sights, did you flirt with anyone?" Or was that in the category of *frivolités?*

"It was a long trip," he nodded. "The food was terrible."

"Well, something sustained you." I looked around the room, bereft of pictures. "Prayer, maybe?"

"There were no services on board—I missed that. The first time I ever ate Christian food was during that trip. But you know what it says in the Talmud: 'You are not allowed to jeopardize your health.'" He seemed uneasy still at this primordial sin, even though since then he had consumed countless businessmen's lunches.

In between the descriptions of food, the sea is calm or he suffers from seasickness, the sun goes down over the mountains in Gibraltar. A young woman dies of typhus and is buried at sea (but in the next sentence he tells us about the wormy cheese and his change of underwear). A woman dentist pulls out his infected tooth without benefit of anaesthetic, and in spite of himself he cries out, "*Maman!*" and regrets his lack of courage.

I look at this old man who doesn't dare tell the doctor of his pain (but he would like to round up dope pushers for a public hanging). My father, who cowered before his superiors all during his work life, now speaks of arming himself with a club to administer lessons in fair play. On the ship he was afraid to transgress the regulation forbidding third-class passengers access to the second-class deck.

"It says here that one night there was music—a violin and mandolin—and that you danced *à la française*." Was it wild abandon, did he have a secret love, was he ever in a fight?

He puts on his glasses—he has grown so thin that they slip off the bridge of his nose. "Yes, I wrote that. Look, the handwriting is not so bad. Maybe you can do something with it," he says vaguely. "For history. The way it was in the old days."

"History?" I laugh. A day by day description of what he ate?

He flips through the pages. "It was interesting," he says, more to himself. "I thought you could—if you want to—"

He wants me to create him as he never was. This twenty-year-old still wet behind the ears who manfully thanks his sister for packing his valise and promises to send for the family once he has a job in America. My grandfather hugs him so forcefully that the bristles of his whiskers dig into my father's cheeks. But my father wishes—in the subjunctive—for the pain to remain as an eternal reminder of his family.

"I used to know a lot of French poetry by heart," he says suddenly. Visiting hours are over and the nurse has entered. "Listen," he says. "'*Heureux qui comme*

136

Ulysse, a fait un beau voyage . . .'" but in full alexan-drine the nurse shoves a thermometer into his mouth.

He waves me out impatiently. He does not like being seen like this, helpless.

Hardly the Ulysses who went on a fine voyage or, as the poem continues, the conqueror of the Golden Fleece who later returned full of wisdom and experience . . .

Perhaps, like a ship's log, the diary contained a message waiting to be deciphered in light of later events. Meanwhile, I thought, I must bring him flowers next time. As though I were welcoming a new arrival.

A Case of Dementia

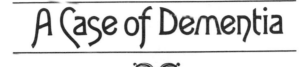

My father, who is not given to introspection except about his pension plan, came to believe that my mother was having a breakdown.

How did he reach this conclusion? His prior experiences with breakdowns were mechanically or municipally related: toasters, subways, the work ethic of civil servants. Within his category of mental aberrations, disrespect for one's parents or husband ranked high.

He whispered over the telephone and I had to strain to hear. Mother had been "hysterical." She had called him names: "tyrant," "dictator," "monster."

In a household where contrariness on the part of its females was regarded as a sign of grippe (the culprit was offered a glass of water and made to lie down), outright criticism was unthinkable. I feared for my father's sanity; Mother was on the road to health. With delight I pictured the scene. Mother brandishing a pot in which she had cooked thousands of delicacies for him, or waving a slipper or—most appalling—rending her clothes after the fashion of her Egyptian countrywomen.

She used to tell me stories about the Arab quarter, the bazaar, the harems, the Arabic girls who taught her to put *kohl* in her eyes and henna in her hair and amulets around her neck. She swore to me that she had given up her Egyptian ways the moment she touched Ellis Island. But I wondered. Her eyes were so large, so dark. She could play the tambourine and gyrate demurely in a rudimentary belly dance.

And now, forty years of submission to my father had finally erupted, accelerated by his retirement. A man who had commanded a large staff on three continents was now reduced to questioning my mother on the wisdom of refrigerating a grapefruit and interrogating her about every telephone call she made or received. To a man who had championed raises for his staff (but not coffee breaks), the sight of Mother leaving him in the middle of the day to attend a meeting of the charitable organization of which she was president constituted dereliction of duty.

I asked if I might speak to her. I wanted to congratulate her. For her benefit, he said heartily, "Everything is fine, fine." Then again in a whisper, "Don't say anything." Then, "Honey, it's your beloved daughter," a curiously archaic mode of referring to me.

"Leave me alone." I heard Mother's voice in the background. "Leave me in peace."

"Everything is under control," my father said loudly. Then, "*Ne dis rien*," as though, along with her reason, she had also lost one of her mother tongues.

To me Mother said, "Is this a life?"

Ignoring the question, I said that it was all to the good that she had finally exploded.

"I'm sick. It was terrible."

"Yes, but—"

"I was tearing my hair," she added, as if to convince me of her dementia. She had in fact said to me recently and quite cheerfully that I must not be surprised if she should go berserk. "Berserk," she had repeated, relishing this exotic word that she knew only from newspaper accounts about seemingly normal persons like herself. "This is Alcatraz," she said, perhaps confusing the George Washington Bridge, which she could see from her window, with the Golden Gate. Earlier she had prepared a six-course meal for my father, with instructions, before leaving for a meeting. He had accused her of abandoning him and threatened to go on his own to the old-age home. "I prepare everything for him. Hand and foot . . . Is this the thanks? No, I don't want coffee now—" He must have made her some, a peace offering. "Half a cup then. Hmm. Not bad. So how are you?" she asked me. "You're lucky. You can come and go as you please. Women's lib."

"Women's lib," Father echoed gaily over the extension phone. "Didn't I just make her a cup of coffee?"

"For better, for worse, and this is worse," he complained when next I phoned. "Of course I didn't say anything, I didn't want to upset her. Monday a meeting, Tuesday a benefit, Wednesday a luncheon—"

What energy, I thought, picturing Mother in her rakish felt hat, those great dark eyes, the snappy leather briefcase.

"What would public opinion say? A wife who leaves home every day. I ask you, is this natural? She is so high-strung. What should I do?" And lest I think he was actually consulting me, he said, "I will speak to the rabbi."

Ah, not that. An unctuous, platitudinous man whose yeshiva was Madison Avenue. But so great was my father's reverence for "the office" that it did not matter what kind of person filled it as long as he displayed the appurtenances. I pictured Claude Rains, *The Invisible Man*, playing the part, skullcap bobbing merrily, prayer shawl sweeping the furniture. Respect for the office was what mattered to my father. Thus when President Nixon was forced to resign, my father felt sorry for him. After all, he was The President. The only office exempt from respect was that of Labor Leader, for to my father it was synonymous with Racketeer, his memory still fresh from the unionization of his clerical staff. This rabbi had already proven himself a keen judge of the human heart by recommending a Caribbean cruise to an insurance agent whose wife's derangement was clearly manifested in her refusal to prepare a box lunch for him every day.

How was mental illness treated in the old country, in Turkey, Greece, Egypt? The afflicted person was said to have had the evil eye cast upon him or her. By having a special incantation performed, the person lost the hex and was cured. The incantation, in Hebrew and Ladino, was first a recitation of all the victim's maternal forbears, followed by a heavily symbolic story about the prophet Eliahu. The person administering the spell must always be a female. It must be learned not through instruction, but through eavesdropping while it is being performed. If the woman reciting it begins to yawn uncontrollably, the spell is working. During my childhood it had been performed with great efficacy by my mother as an all-purpose cure, equally good for melancholia and viral infections, though over the years it had gradually been replaced by penicillin.

One day I discovered, tucked into the drawer where I kept my tennis socks, a gaudy glass bead that I recognized as the charm against the evil eye. It was crudely painted with concentric circles, in the middle of which was a blue dot, presumably the iris, rimmed in (bloodshot) red, the whole resembling a bulging eye suffering from glaucoma. Designed to outstare the evil eye, it had been hidden there for my protection by my mother.

To my father's great relief, the rabbi renders the verdict that my mother is suffering from overwork and needs to curtail her activities outside the home. "Psychiatry, shmuckiatry," my father says. "A racket. They make money so families can split up. Look at the divorce rate."

I look and wonder how my parents have stayed together for so long. Was she ever truly happy? Was he ever different? Always the despot, benevolent but always contemptuous of any ambition she might have entertained (though he boasted of her capabilities behind her back). A woman who might have gone to college or held an important position. Now she administers thousands of dollars, supervises dozens of volunteers, a woman who writes and edits reports, deals with printers, rabbis, caterers, immigrants, and bureaucrats. Why has it taken her so long to revolt?

"Everything is under control," he says in the middle of our phone conversation, signaling my mother's arrival home. "How's the weather there?" as though I were in Palm Beach instead of three miles downtown. "Darling, I was just saying that your daughter is almost as pretty as you." He laughs that nasty laugh I've heard so often.

"This is not a life," she says to me, answering her own question from an earlier conversation. "You know your mother is nothing but a vegetable? Come for dinner or I won't be responsible . . ."

No help for it. I leave my office early and rush uptown to pay my call on the unhinged woman.

A barefoot woman opens the door and greets me by

singing a song in Italian. Not Hello, glad to see you, but instead a song about a sprig of violets plucked from a mountainside, sung in a strained alto—she has never reconciled herself to being a soprano manquée. She is braless and disheveled, her slip hangs down below a crooked hem. She sashays across the room, ending her song, and with scarcely a pause for breath, starts reciting a long poem in French about a noble wolf. On the table there is food for ten though we are only three tonight. One never knows who will drop in, and truth to say, in the old days people were always dropping in and staying. "Is this my daughter?" she asks after ending her poem, upon which my father gives me a meaningful look.

A loud street noise startles us and Mother quickly licks her index finger and touches her throat three times, uttering a few expletives in Arabic.

"Isn't she cute," Father says to me with an agonized smile.

Mother points to him. "Dr. Jekyll and Mr. Hyde."

I am very relieved. There is nothing untoward in her behavior. She is quite herself. "How like yourself you are," I say, quoting Strindberg to her.

"I knew you would understand." Tucking her arm under mine she says, "Only what is written in French is poetry, and only what is sung in Italian is music. The rest is holy — the Hebrew — or harsh — the German." Her cultural cosmos has no room for the Scandinavians.

"Strindberg was a Swede, Mom."

"Smorgasbord," she says, leading me to the kitchen.

"When do we eat?" Father taps on a glass with a fork. "Let's have a little service around here."

"Do you know that he can't even boil water?" Mother asks.

"What good is boiled water?" he says.

"*A boire, à boire, par pitié!*" she cries. A drink, a drink, for pity's sake. Father pours some wine. And not to be outdone, recites a short poem in French about a shipwreck. The dinner ends with conviviality. They appear to be making eyes at each other, and I leave soon after dinner, not wishing to be *de trop*.

Distraught, my father has violated the hallowed custom of the parent waiting for the child to call and phones me to say that in his time women were stoned for desertion.

"Desertion? You mean adultery."

She phoned him from the *street* and refused to say where she was.

We must call the police. This is alarming.

"All she said was she had a ticket."

"A ticket? Train, bus, plane—?"

"A matinee. I ask you, is this right? Without consultation?"

"Without permission you mean," I say, emboldened.

"Of course I would have given my permission. I am a reasonable man. I don't know what to do any more."

"Perhaps—" dare I say it? "—it would be good for you to talk to a psychiatrist."

"God forbid. Charlatans. They are worse than chiropractors. They are all in cahoots. No. I have an idea. You are going to laugh at it." He hesitates while I clear my throat. "My father, may he rest in peace, would turn over in his grave if he were alive. But I am a desperate man."

Not a Caribbean cruise.

Not garlic hung around the neck.

Not a walnut shell inscribed with Hebrew characters, to be placed under a pillow.

His solution is that I, the daughter, must perform the evil-eye exorcism upon my mother. Ah no—this is the twentieth century. I remember myself as a scoffing, irreverent child, sick with stomach aches, chicken pox, strep throat; giggling as my mother performed it at my bedside, tolerant and loving even as I mimicked her yawning.

"Really, Dad—"

"It worked for you, didn't it? You got rid of the measles. And when I had pleurisy . . ."

Yes, this is our answer to the Ashkenazim. The evil-eye incantation in lieu of chicken soup. "But I don't know it. I never memorized it."

"If you are not willing to help your own mother. . ."

"All right, but it's absurd. In this day and age." My bravado masks the strain of superstition that prevents me from ever breaking a chain letter (*The last person who broke this chain suffered a cerebral hemorrhage*). Why take a chance?

One late afternoon, a stylish woman in her mid-thirties, dressed in a suit and carrying an attaché case hurries to—a board meeting? A conference? A senate subcommittee hearing or a lecture hall to address a gathering?

This woman is going to cast a hex over the evil eye. Not in a village hovel or a stucco house with no plumbing overlooking the Mediterranean, but in a thirty-five-story apartment house with the thin walls, plastic palms, and peeling paint that are *de rigueur* in new buildings. Closed-circuit television reveals to the doorman a professional woman of the new breed, the kind who understands corporate law and makes decisions affecting his life. The woman's lips are moving. She is babbling a spell whose origins are lost in twelfth-century Spain.

The victim opens the door cheerfully. How to reconcile polyester with exorcism? Is there a connection? Mother shrugs. "If it will make him happy. . . I threw him out. We can't have a man listening. What a lovely evening. What a shame to stay home. I would rather go to Lord and Taylor. You need a new raincoat. Why do you wear such dark colors?" She fingers my suit. I am reminded of my father's "You are almost as pretty as your mother."

"Now, Mom, you know I think this is ridiculous. All this ancient mumbo jumbo."

This unleashes a monologue in French by Racine, about honoring one's ancestors, all while she plies me with food.

148

"And besides," she finishes, "it always worked when
I did it."

I pick up the gauntlet and stamp around. "Well I
suppose it can't hurt."

We lower the blinds and take the telephone off the hook.
I feel as though I am about to perform the Black Mass.
Mother lies down on her bed. The Arts and Leisure
section from last Sunday's *Times* is on her night table,
along with a dog-eared copy of proverbs by La
Rochefoucauld.

"Salt," she prompts me.

I go into the kitchen and pour about half a tea-
spoonful into my right hand.

Mother's eyes are closed. Will something dreadful
happen if I don't do it right? *The last person who broke
the chain died a horrible death.*

"Take your time, honey," she says. "I'm very comfortable."

I raise my right hand and make a pass over her face.
I begin to recite in Ladino, with my American accent:
"*Vida, daughter of Allegra, whose mother was Miriam . . .*"
I feel a lump in my throat. I am blessing my mother.
"*Before her was Fortuna who was the fruit of Esther . . .*"
A veritable Amazon land from which men are excluded.
Women's lib, I hear my father say. Mother sighs. Words
come into my head, Hebrew blessings learned as an
unwilling Sunday school student. I am swaying now as I
chant. Twenty floors below us, trucks rattle down the
avenue, a few bars of disco music float up and die away.

There is a smile on Mother's face, her eyes remain closed. Now again in Ladino: *"Eliahu walked down the road, clad in iron, shod in iron. Three keys he carried: one to open the gate, one to lock it, and one to ward off the evil eye."* I smother a yawn and repeat the line about the three keys. I see him clanking down a country road, dusty trees—poplars, cypresses—the prophet in medieval garb, fooling the authorities, fooling the evil eye, casting away doubt and evil from the people of Israel. *"How many are the daughters, how many are the names, how many are the signs and wonders?"* I am so tired. I can hardly raise the hand holding the salt over Mother's face. Wearily, yawning, I trace a six-pointed star across her face, a name for each point of the star, a blessing for each name, miracles for each succeeding generation, a logarithmic explosion of miracles for my mother.

She opens her eyes and nods kindly at me, at my hand. I open it, press the index finger of my left hand to the salt so that some grains adhere to it. She sits up and I place my finger gently in her mouth, applying the salt to her palate. I do this three times, reciting a three-fold blessing in Hebrew that I do not remember ever having heard before. My eyes are tearing. Violently I throw the salt over her left shoulder. I am yawning uncontrollably. Mother reaches out and embraces me.

"How do you feel?" I ask, not knowing what to do with the rest of the salt on my palm.

"Wonderful," she says. "For once your father was right. I never felt better in my life."

8/2000

RETOLD MYTHS SERIES

RETOLD AFRICAN MYTHS

RETOLD CLASSIC MYTHS
VOLUME 1

RETOLD CLASSIC MYTHS
VOLUME 2

RETOLD CLASSIC MYTHS
VOLUME 3

RETOLD WORLD MYTHS

Perfection Learning Corporation, Logan, Iowa 51546

RETOLD MYTHS SERIES

RETOLD AFRICAN MYTHS®

ELEANORA E. TATE

PERFECTION LEARNING

Editor-in-Chief:
Kathleen Myers

Managing Editor:
Beth Obermiller

Senior Editor:
Marsha James

Editors:
Christine LePorte
Cecelia Munzenmaier
Terry Ofner

Cover and Inside Illustration:
Don Tate

Layout Design:
Don Tate

ABOUT THE AUTHOR

Eleanora E. Tate

Eleanora E. Tate, a native of Canton, Missouri, has been a professional writer for over 25 years. Her first young adult novel, *Just an Overnight Guest*, was adapted in 1983 into an award-winning movie of the same name.

Her second book, *Secret of Gumbo Grove*, won the Parents' Choice Gold Seal Award in 1987. It was also nominated for a 1991-92 California Young Readers Medal Award.

Ms. Tate has been interested in myths and storytelling for many years. In 1982, she traveled through Europe researching ethnic folktales, and she is the current president of the National Association of Black Storytellers, Inc. Ms. Tate lives in Morehead City, North Carolina.

ABOUT THE ARTIST

Don Tate II

Don Tate has been designing and illustrating books and educational products for the past 10 years.

Don likes to explore various artistic styles and mediums so that he can match his artistic mood to the mood of the project. Don gained his inspiration for the illustrations in this book by researching African art and sculpture.

Don Tate lives in Des Moines, Iowa. He divides his time between his art projects and his family.

AUTHOR'S PREFACE

The stories in *Retold African Myths* are my literary "inspirations" of age-old tales that have existed for centuries, primarily in oral form. Perfection Learning and its consultants researched and selected the variants which are the basis of the stories in this collection. After this process, the editors invited me to retell the selected versions in my own style and voice.

My objective was not to "improve" the original tales. This would be an impossible goal. Instead, I tried to come to an understanding of the intent and language of the stories in my own way. The result is stories written from unique points of view with a few added characters and situations.

Hopefully, my "inspired" stories will be looked upon as my sincere and humble attempt to pay homage to the legacy of our truly great African myths, folklore, and legends; and to adolescent reading and literacy.

Eleanora E. Tate

TABLE

OF CONTENTS

WELCOME TO THE RETOLD AFRICAN MYTHS®

In Africa, the myths in this book would probably not be read. Rather, they would be told. There is a rich and varied tradition of storytelling in Africa—as rich and varied as the continent of Africa itself. This tradition is full of celebration, humor, and entertainment.

But myths aren't only for entertainment. They also carry on a culture's values from generation to generation. A story about how a heroine faces down a deadly snake helps define strength and goodness. And thrift and generosity are taught when a character creates a disaster through laziness or greed.

The myths in this volume can also serve as a kind of encyclopedia. By reading these myths, you can learn what various cultures think and believe. For example, myths show how early Africans explained the mysteries of life and nature. Why do bats sleep upside down in caves? How did human life begin? Why do people die? The myths in this book provide fascinating answers to such questions.

Finally, these myths are simply great stories. Filled with drama, beauty, and humor, they still attract listeners long after they were first told.

RETOLD UPDATE

This book presents a collection of eighteen adapted myths from the African continent. All the variety, excitement, and humorous details of the original versions are here.

In addition, a word list has been added at the beginning of each story. Each word defined on that list is printed in dark type within the story. If you forget the meaning of one of these words, just check the list to review the definition.

You'll also find footnotes at the bottom of some story

pages. These notes identify people or places, explain ideas, show pronunciations, or provide cultural information.

We offer two other features you may wish to use. One is a map of Africa on the following page. This map locates the region where each of the myths was originally told.

You will also find more cultural information in the Insights sections after each myth. These revealing facts will add to your understanding of the different ways of life in Africa.

One last word. Since many of these myths and stories have been handed down for centuries, several versions exist. So a story you read here will probably differ from a version you read elsewhere.

But that's all part of the tradition. Each storyteller is expected to add something new to the old tales. You may even want to read some of these stories aloud. Adding sound effects and acting out parts will help you come closer to the experience of African storytelling.

The oldest known African myth was first told 2,000 years ago. Now it's your turn to read and retell these timeless stories.

Key to Cultural Groups

1. Ashanti

2. Bambara

3. Chagga

4. Ganda

5. Hausa

6. Kono

7. Mende

8. Sotho

9. Swahili

10. Yoruba

11. Zulu

CREATION

How Nambi Gained Her Beloved

Obatala Creates the World

Heart Finds a Home

Creation myths are told throughout Africa. Each traditional cultural group tells its own stories of how life began. None of these tales are exactly alike, but they all do one thing. They tell of a supreme god who made the universe.

The Supreme God knows everything. But he is sometimes confusing to humans. For example, he does good things for people, but he can send evil into the world as well.

The Supreme God is known by many different names throughout the continent. In eastern Africa, the Supreme God is usually called Mulungu. Central Africans refer to him as Leza. In the west, he is known as Nyambi. To the Yoruba peoples of Nigeria, the Supreme God is Olorun. You will meet Olorun in the second myth in this section.

HOW NAMBI GAINED HER BELOVED

VOCABULARY PREVIEW

Below is a list of words that appear in the story. Read the list and get to know the words before you read the story.

bore—gave birth to
edible—able to be eaten
ravenous—very hungry
relented—gave in
resourceful—clever; skillful
scornful—critical; doubtful
sustenance—food; nourishment
willful—stubborn

Main Characters

Bee—friend of Nambi
Gulu—sky god
Kaizuki—oldest son of Gulu
Kintu—first man
Nambi—daughter of Gulu
Walumbe—son of Gulu

Gods and humans usually kept their distance—that is, until Kintu and Nambi fell in love. While Kintu was only a man, Nambi was the daughter of the great sky god. Could a bee help Kintu pass the sky god's tests so that the two lovers could be united?

How Nambi Gained Her Beloved

Adapted from a tale of Uganda

In the first days, the goddess Nambi[1] lived in heaven. She lived there with her father, Gulu,[2] the sky god. Her two brothers—Walumbe and Kaizuki[3]—lived in heaven as well.

[1] (nam´ bē)
[2] (gu´ lu)
[3] (wal um´ bā) (ka ē zu´ kē)

One day Nambi decided to visit earth. Now Nambi was sometimes **willful** and independent. So Gulu sent her brother Walumbe to watch after her.

Soon after Nambi and Walumbe stepped on earth, they came upon a man sleeping beside his cow. The sleeper was Kintu,[4] the first man. The cow was the First Mother of **Sustenance.** The cow gave Kintu all that he needed to eat.

Upon seeing the man, Nambi fell in love with him. But her brother Walumbe was **scornful.** "You have been made crazy by the sun's blazing rays," he said. "This man has no wealth. Notice, he sleeps on the ground, so he must have no dwelling. His only companion is this cow, so she probably feeds him. Must a lowly cowherd become the husband of the royal daughter of the heavens?"

"Hush up," Nambi said. "And quit talking about his cow."

Nambi woke the man and introduced herself. "I'm Nambi, daughter of the sky god. I want to marry you."

Nambi saw Walumbe frown and added quickly, "But first you must be accepted by my father and my brothers. If you agree, I will come back for you soon."

"I would be honored," replied Kintu with surprise in his voice.

Walumbe fussed all the way home. How could his sister want to marry a human!

Upon their return to heaven, Nambi and Walumbe went to their father, King Gulu. Walumbe was first to speak.

"Nambi wants to marry the first earth man she sees!" he complained. "This marriage would cause us all shame."

King Gulu thought about the problem for a moment. Then he made a decision. "We'll test the man three times," Gulu said to Nambi. "If he passes the tests, I'll let you marry him."

Walumbe came up with the first test. "I want to see how long Kintu can live without his cow," he said to Gulu and Nambi. "I will hide the cow in the royal herd."

And so Walumbe returned to earth and stole Kintu's cow. He hid it in Gulu's royal herd in heaven.

[4] (kin´ tu)

Nambi watched from above while Kintu searched for the missing cow. With no milk to drink or cheese to eat, he soon grew **ravenous.** Nambi decided to help her beloved. So she sent a friendly bee from the royal pasture down to earth.

But when Kintu spied the bee, he tried to kill it for food. "You haven't been in the habit of eating living things," Bee said. "You don't have to start with me. There's plenty of food all around you. Follow me."

The bee flew about and showed Kintu the plants he could eat. In this way humans first learned about **edible** plants. And Kintu was able to live without his cow. So he passed his first test.

Gulu was impressed. "Your man is very **resourceful,**" he told Nambi. "You may return to earth and bring Kintu to heaven for a visit."

Walumbe was disappointed that Kintu had passed the first test. "But he won't pass the next one!" he told himself.

Walumbe was the first to greet Nambi and Kintu when they returned to heaven. "Welcome," Walumbe told Kintu with a smile. "In your behalf, our servants have prepared a feast for you."

Then Walumbe led Kintu into a large room. Kintu was surprised to see tables covered with breads, vegetables, and fruits of all kinds.

"This must be another test," Nambi whispered to Kintu. "Walumbe will watch to see if you can eat all the food. If not, the wedding will be called off."

Walumbe smiled again and made his sister leave the room. Then he locked the door. Kintu was left to eat all the food by himself.

Kintu ate and ate and ate, but there was still food left. After much worrying, he thought to pull back the mat on the floor. Seeing a loose board, he quickly pulled it up. There was space below. Kintu dropped all the food into the hole and replaced the board.

King Gulu and Nambi's other brother, Kaizuki, were pleased when they saw Kintu seated at the empty table. Walumbe, however, was furious. He persuaded Gulu and

Kaizuki to let him put Kintu to the third and last test.

"See this rock?" said Walumbe, holding up a large stone. "Our father requires special fuel for his fires. Chop fuel from this rock."

"Walumbe, you're being very unfair," Nambi said.

Gulu interrupted. "The man who becomes your husband will have to be extra smart. You see who he'll have to put up with!"

Nambi **relented** and sadly led Kintu away. She was sure Kintu would fail the last test. But Kintu was not ready to give up.

Taking an ax, Kintu wedged the blade into tiny cracks in the rock. Patiently he wiggled the blade back and forth. Rock chips finally fell to the ground. Kintu then mixed the chips with tree bark.

"I have brought you fuel for your fire," Kintu said respectfully to Gulu. And when Kintu tossed the rock and bark into Gulu's royal fire, flames burst up.

Nambi and Kaizuki applauded. "Kintu, you have my blessing and my daughter," Gulu said.

"But wait," Walumbe said in a loud voice. "Don't forget your cow, Kintu. You wouldn't want to return to earth without her, would you?"

"I was about to discuss the sacredness of marriage, Walumbe," Gulu said. "Can't the cow wait?"

"Let's take care of this small matter first," Walumbe said quickly.

"There he goes again," Nambi whispered. "All of those cows look alike. If you choose the wrong one, you'll look foolish. Walumbe will persuade my father to not let us wed."

But Kintu was not left helpless. As Walumbe led him to the royal pasture, the friendly bee lit on Kintu's ear. "Watch me carefully," Bee said. "I'll show you which one is your cow. Then I'll show you her new calves too."

Kintu watched the bee as the first herd of cows was paraded by. But Bee didn't move. "My cow isn't in this herd," Kintu said confidently.

Kintu again shook his head as the second herd was led by.

But when the third herd walked by, Bee lit on a cow's tail. "This is my cow," Kintu declared. Bee went on to light on two small calves. "And these are her calves that she **bore** while here."

"You are indeed a smart man," said Gulu with admiration. "You may marry my daughter. Welcome to the family!"

So Nambi and Kintu were wed and left that day to start their new life on earth.

This is how the first man and first woman came into the world. This is also why people and bees are good friends and live in harmony.

As for Walumbe, he lived to create more problems for Kintu and Nambi. Perhaps someday you will hear more of the story.

INSIGHTS

The story of Kintu and Nambi is part of an epic told in Buganda—one of the regions of Uganda in central Africa. This epic tells of the brave deeds of Kintu, the founder of Buganda.

Most epics are based on actual people and events. But as the story is retold, the human characters can become almost godlike. That is what happened to Kintu.

In the Buganda epic, Kintu was the first man. In history he was the first king of Uganda.

Before the historical Kintu was born, the tribes in Uganda were small and scattered. Kintu gathered them into one nation. People respected him so much that they said he was descended from the gods.

According to tradition, King Kintu didn't have a wife. The god Gulu saw that the king was lonely. So Gulu gave Kintu his own daughter—Nambi.

After Kintu died, the legend of his many deeds lived on. All the kings of Uganda claim they are related to the great Kintu.

OBATALA CREATES THE WORLD

VOCABULARY PREVIEW

Below is a list of words that appear in the story. Read the list and get to know the words before you read the story.

consult—talk with; ask for advice
descent—downward movement
disfigured—deformed; imperfect
domain—land belonging to a ruler
potential—possibilities; promise
thatched—covered with leaves or other plant materials

Main Characters

Chameleon—messenger for the Supreme God
Obatala—god who made humans
Olokun—goddess of the marshes
Olorun—Supreme God
Orunmila—god who knows the future; Olorun's son

When the heavens were made, the earth didn't exist. Most of the gods were content with this plan. But young Obatala was bored. He wanted things to be different. So he set out to find what he could make.

OBATALA CREATES THE WORLD

Adapted from a Yoruba tale

In the beginning of Yoruba Time, all things waited to be made or improved upon. There was heaven—where the gods lived—and water below it. But there was no solid ground. No sun shone down upon the mists. And there were no people to laugh or work below the sky.

The goddess Olokun[1] ruled the grayness hanging between the water and heaven. All the mists and marshes belonged to her. She liked things the way they were in her **domain.**

But Obatala[2]—one of the younger gods— thought things were too empty. All those mists and gray clouds bored Obatala. So the young god

[1] (ōl´ō kun)
[2] (ōb a tal´ a)

formed a plan. Then he went to talk to the Supreme God, Olorun.[3]

It was Olorun who ruled the sky and all the other gods and goddesses. He too was satisfied with things as they were.

But the Supreme God had a soft spot for the energetic Obatala. In fact, the two gods could have been father and son—they were that close. So when Obatala begged to speak to Olorun, the Supreme God listened.

Obatala eagerly began explaining his idea. "If I had my way, I could do some wonderful things with Olokun's marshes and swamps," he announced. "I could create solid land down there, with dry fields and forests.

"Just think," he continued enthusiastically, "we could all live down there! It would be a great thing for us. Goddess Olokun simply doesn't realize the **potential** of what she has."

The Supreme God smiled at Obatala. "As always, Obatala, you're full of interesting ideas."

"I have your permission then?" Obatala asked quickly.

Olorun nodded. "You may begin," he said. "But first talk to my son Orunmila.[4] He can help you. Tell him that I sent you."

Now the god Orunmila was a wise diviner.[5] The future held no secrets from him, and he knew the mystery of all things.

Obatala went immediately to **consult** Orunmila about his plan. Orunmila let the excited younger god talk himself out.

After Obatala was finished, the diviner said, "You'll need to make a chain of gold. This chain must reach from the sky down to the waters."

"A chain of gold," Obatala repeated excitedly. "What else?"

"Fill a snail shell with sand. Then find a white hen, a black cat, and a palm nut. Put all of these things in a bag. When you climb down the golden chain, take the bag with you."

---

[3] (ōl´ ōr un)
[4] (ōr un mil´ a)
[5] A diviner is a person who tells the future. Diviners are still a part of Yoruba culture.

Obatala thanked Orunmila and left to round up all the gold he could find. He took it to the goldsmith, who just shook his head. "You'll hang in the air for a long time if this is all the gold you have," the goldsmith warned.

"It's the best I could do," Obatala told him. "Do what you can with what I gave you. And please be sure to put a hook at one end of the chain."

When the goldsmith finished his work, Obatala and Orunmila went to the end of the sky. There Obatala fastened the hook of the chain to the sky's edge.

Next, Obatala wrapped the bag around his wrist. Then saying farewell to Orunmila, the young god gripped the chain and began his **descent.**

Time passed. As Obatala climbed lower, the light dimmed. Finally it got so gray he couldn't see a thing. But he could hear waves as they crashed against each other in the sea below. Then Obatala came to the end of the chain.

"I may be a god, but I can't swim," Obatala thought as he dangled from the chain. He hung there for a long time, thinking and worrying. Then, from far above, Obatala heard Orunmila's voice.

"What did you say?" he shouted back.

"The sand," Orunmila called down. "Pour the sand from the shell into the water."

"What good will that do?" Obatala hollered back.

"Just do what I say," Orunmila told him.

Obatala obeyed.

"Now the hen," said Orunmila.

"The hen?" thought Obatala. He opened his mouth to argue. But his arms were getting tired. Maybe it was a crazy idea, but it was better than falling into the sea.

"The hen," commanded Orunmila. "Free the white hen!"

Obatala pulled the hen from the bag. With a cluck and a flutter, the hen flapped down to the water. She scratched at the sand with her feet, scattering the sand in all directions. And wherever the sand fell, hills and valleys formed.

Obatala let go of the chain and fell to the new land. Earth stretched everywhere. There was promise of more new things to come.

The young god's first action was to plant the palm nut. Immediately a palm tree sprang up and quickly grew to its full height.

Next Obatala used the bark of the palm to build a small house. He then **thatched** a roof for his house using the tree's leaves. Obatala stood back and admired his work.

"I name this place Ife, meaning 'wide,' and Ile,[6] meaning 'house,'" Obatala said.

This is how Ile-Ife, the most sacred city of the Yoruba people, came to be.

After some time had passed, the Supreme God Olorun sent his messenger, Chameleon, down to check on Obatala.

Chameleons, as you know, take on the color of whatever object they are near. So as soon as Chameleon touched the chain, he turned a golden color. He sparkled and glittered during his long descent to Ile-Ife.

Obatala noticed the bright glitter coming toward him. He soon recognized Chameleon and invited the messenger into his home.

Chameleon sat on the grass mat. He immediately turned a brilliant emerald green.

"The Great Olorun sent me," said Chameleon. "He wants to know how you are doing."

"As you can see, we have a fine beginning," Obatala told him. "But it is awfully gray down here. Could you ask the Great Olorun to make it brighter?"

Chameleon returned to Olorun with Obatala's request. The Supreme God immediately created the sun and rolled it across the sky. Ile-Ife was bathed in warm, golden light.

With the creation of the sun, all was well in Ile-Ife. All was well except that Obatala was lonely. He needed someone to talk to. Therefore he decided to create beings who could share his new world.

Obatala didn't have much to work with. So he began cre-

---

[6] (ē´ fay) (ē´ lay) Ife is a city in western Nigeria.

ating tiny figures out of mud. He shaped figures who looked a good deal like himself.

But Obatala's work made him thirsty. He took a break to drink some wine made from palm juice. Unfortunately the wine made his brain and fingers clumsy. When he returned to work, several pieces slipped from his hands and became **disfigured.**

Obatala laid his figures in the sun to dry. But he didn't notice the misshapen people. When he finished, he called to the Supreme God. "Great Olorun, only you can breathe life into what I have made. If they are pleasing to you, bring my people to life."

Instantly Obatala's creations changed into real people.

Happy with his work, Obatala found his way to his house. There he slept off the palm wine.

When Obatala awoke, he was alarmed to find several imperfect people. One that fell on his leg had a bent leg. One that fell on his head spent all his time thinking.

Looking at them made the god sorrowful. From that day, he vowed never to touch wine again. Obatala also became the protector of all people born with imperfections.

This is how all life came to be.

INSIGHTS

The Yoruba people have a long history dating back to around 300 B.C. At that time they developed several city-states near the Niger River. About ten million Yoruba still live in this area of Nigeria.

Today, many Yoruba follow the Christian or Muslim religions. But believers in the traditional Yoruba ways say they are descended from Orunmila, the diviner. A diviner is someone who foretells the future. As in the myth, a Yoruba diviner usually doesn't make detailed predictions. Rather, he suggests the best way to act or warns against dangers. His advice helps people understand the will of the gods.

Many Yoruba households have a shrine to this god, who is also known as the god of knowledge.

In the myth, a goldsmith makes Obatala's chain for him. This goldsmith is actually Ogun, the god of iron.

Ogun is still worshipped by the Yoruba—especially anyone who works with metal. In fact, some truck drivers always pray to Ogun before a trip. Otherwise, they believe Ogun might cause an accident while they are driving.

We saw in the myth how Obatala was able to form human beings from clay. However, only the Supreme God Olorun was able to breathe life into Obatala's clay forms.

Obatala was jealous of Olorun's life-giving power. He was determined to discover Olorun's secret. So one night he hid near some of his human forms to see Olorun at work.

But Olorun knew everything—including Obatala's plan. So before going to work, he put Obatala into a deep sleep. As a result, Obatala never did discover the secret of life.

HEART FINDS A HOME

VOCABULARY PREVIEW

Below is a list of words that appear in the story. Read the list and get to know the words before you read the story.

abode—home; dwelling
agitated—troubled; disturbed
compassion—feeling of tenderness and concern
marveled—wondered; was in awe
mulled—thought over
pledges—promises

Main Characters

High God—creator of all things
First Man
First Woman
Moon
Night   —children of the High God
Rain
Sun
Mutima—Heart

The creator made the world and then went away. Left behind, Mutima was lonely. He searched for the High God until he found an answer to the longing in his heart.

HEART FINDS A HOME

ADAPTED FROM A TALE OF UGANDA

In the earliest of times, God created Earth, Sun, Moon, Night, and Rain. Then God came to Earth and made the First Man and the First Woman.

God didn't stay with his creation long. Soon after all was made, God prepared to return to heaven. But before he left, he created Heart and named him Mutima.[1]

Now Mutima **marveled**

---

[1] (mu tē´ ma)

at all that the highest god had created. The more he marveled, the more he wished he could meet the creator of such wonders. So one day, Mutima went walking in search of the Most High God.

Along the way, Mutima met Rain. He introduced himself.

"I'm looking for the Most High God," said Mutima. "Have you seen him?"

"I haven't seen him for ages," replied Rain.

This news **agitated** Mutima. "Where has God gone?" he asked. "What are we to do without him?"

"His absence makes no difference to me," replied Rain. "I'll just rain until it floods."

"Have mercy," cried Mutima. "Listen, let Sun dry out the land a bit before you rain again. Use a balanced hand."

Rain **mulled** this over and decided that this was good. Mutima and Rain became friends.

Mutima next met Sun. He introduced himself.

"Have you seen the Most High God?" he asked. "I would like to meet him."

"You won't find him around here," replied Sun. "I think he withdrew to heaven."

"Oh, no!" cried Mutima. "What are we to do without him?"

Sun replied, "I hadn't thought much about doing anything else except shine and burn, shine and burn."

"Have pity," said Mutima, with **compassion.** "The people's crops will shrivel up. Listen, after you've warmed the Earth, please give Rain a chance to refresh things a little."

Sun considered Mutima's plea and decided that it was good. They became friends.

Mutima then met Night and Moon and introduced himself to them. He asked Night if she had seen the Most High God.

"He has gone to heaven," Night answered. "His **abode** is farther away than the farthest star."

"This is terrible," said Mutima. "What are we to do?"

"I don't know about you, but it's no problem for me," said Night.

"Why?" asked Mutima. "What are your plans?"

"To keep everything dark, of course."

"Oh, have a heart," said Mutima. "Man and Woman will never see the beautiful Earth that God has created. Night, try this. Share time with Sun and Moon. There's enough room for everyone."

Night thought this over and decided that it was good. Moon was pleased as well. They all became friends.

Sun, Night, Moon, and Rain held to their **pledges.** Night and Moon made their rounds and made room for Sun. After Sun warmed the earth, Rain brought refreshment.

Mutima was glad that he had met the other children of the High God. But he still longed to meet God himself.

Mutima continued walking. Then Mutima saw the First Man and the First Woman planting crops in a field.

"I cannot find God," Mutima said. "But I've found his children."

Opening wide his arms, Mutima greeted the man and woman. He decided to share his heart with them until God came back.

Mutima still lives with the people. And that's why all men and women have compassion. And that's why all people share Mutima's longing for God's return.

INSIGHTS

The story about Mutima, or Heart, is from the Ganda people. The Ganda once ruled the largest kingdom in Africa. Today they are the main cultural group in Uganda. Nearly one million Ganda live northwest of Lake Victoria. Their official religion is Christianity.

As in this story, many African myths tell that the creator once lived on earth. But for one reason or another, he left to live in heaven.

A Mende tradition says that the creator lived on earth with the first people. He allowed the people to ask him for whatever they needed. When they asked for something, he would reply, "Just take it." This happened so often that people thought God's name was "Just Take It."

Finally, the creator got tired of the people's constant demands. So he left to find a place where he wouldn't be bothered.

Another African story tells of a woman who was grinding corn into flour. She was using a club with a long handle. Because of her carelessness, the handle of the club hit the High God in the eye. He got angry and left to find a more peaceful place.

One story says the sky was so close to the earth that people could touch it. At first the High God lived in the sky close to the people. But he left when people started using his beard for a towel.

DEATH

Death and the River King

Walumbe's Revenge

Why Folks Must Die

All cultures have an explanation of why people die and what happens to them after death. In many African myths, the first men and women were to live forever. But then death came into the world because of a mistake or an accident.

The myths in this section give three versions of how death came to live here on earth.

DEATH AND THE RIVER KING

VOCABULARY PREVIEW

Below is a list of words that appear in the story. Read the list and get to know the words before you read the story.

barbs—insults
eternal—never-ending
miserable—poor
protruding—sticking out of the surface of an object
regal—kingly; dignified; noble
rivalry—competition
trespass—enter; intrude

Main Characters

Death
Hunter
Tano—river god

There once was a man who was a terrible hunter. One day he came upon an antelope. Taking a deep breath, he let fly his best shot. Little did the man know that his fateful arrow would bring death into the world.

DEATH

AND THE RIVER KING

Inspired by a tale from the people of Togo

There was once a man who was a terrible hunter. He rarely found game. When he did, he lost the tracks and the animal escaped.

Since the man's aim was as bad as his tracking, he rarely hit any-thing. You see, when he shot arrows to the left, they flew off to the right. When he shot to the right, they flew off to the left.

One morning the man saw an antelope drinking from the river near his village. He was so excited, he almost dropped his bow. But he took a deep breath and let fly his best shot.

The hunter had aimed to the left, so of course, his arrow sailed off to the right. But listen! The antelope bounded away—to the right! And the man's arrow actually plunged into the antelope's side!

The antelope sped away, leaping into a clump of bushes along the riverbank. The happy hunter jumped after the antelope. Thump! He landed in a clearing.

What he saw there filled him with amazement and fear. He found no antelope. Instead he beheld the mighty river god Tano.[1] And an arrow was **protruding** from his thigh.

The frightened man fell to his knees. "Oh, my Lord, I beg your mercy!" he cried. "I didn't know it was you. Oh, please, forgive me. I'll never hunt again."

Tano pulled the arrow from his thigh. "I've watched your **miserable** hunting for many years. How you were able to shoot me, neither of us will ever understand. Stand up, hunter. I'm not harmed."

The man, however, stayed on his knees. He begged and begged Tano's pardon. Then to show his complete goodwill, the hunter invited Tano to his home.

"I only have a simple meal of bread, fruit, and yams," the hunter said. "But you're welcome to all I have."

Tano was touched by the invitation and accepted. But just as Tano and the hunter turned toward the man's home, up jumped Death.

"And where do you go, River God?" Death asked in a firm voice.

"To visit my new friend, if you must know," Tano replied.

"But to do that, you must cross over *my* land," said Death. "You can't do that without my permission. You may rule the water, but I rule the land."

You see, Death and Tano had a long-standing **rivalry.** Death was in charge of the land, while Tano controlled the

---

[1] (ta´ nō)

water. But each one was always trying to **trespass** on the other's territory.

"You have no authority to order us around," Tano declared. "We go where we please."

Death held up his hand in a warning. "You should keep me happy. I have ways of getting what I want. You may not step on my land without my permission. And *I* don't give permission!"

Tano hesitated. Then he sat down on a log to think over his enemy's words. But shortly he stood up and faced Death.

> My name is Tano, River King,
> And I go wherever I please.
> You got about as much rule over me
> As a hyena[2] has over its fleas.

Death frowned up at Tano. He crossed his arms and stroked his chin. Just as Tano and the hunter started past him again, Death shouted,

> Stop! You may be Tano and you may be king.
> But with Brother Death, that don't mean a thing.
> The land is mine; you better do as I say.
> With Death in charge, there's no other way.

Tano cut in,

> You talk up a streak,
> But your words are cheap.
> Move out of the way;
> I got appointments to keep.

And so it went back and forth, each one stopping the other with words. They kept it up for two days and two nights. Finally Tano and Death ran out of insults and comebacks. The two gods sat in silence, searching their memories for fresh **barbs.**

---

[2] A hyena is a large doglike mammal.

Finally the hunter got up and said in a tired voice, "You two go ahead. I'm heading home to get something to eat."

"Okay, okay!" said Death. "Let's try this. Whoever reaches the hunter's home first can be his guest for dinner and spend the night."

Tano quickly agreed. He and the hunter went one way. Death went another.

Being ruler over the land, Death was convinced he could reach the hunter's hut first. But the hunter knew of a shortcut, so he and his **regal** guest arrived first.

Tano was waiting at the entrance of the hunter's compound[3] when Death ran up, all out of breath. With a playful smile, Tano poked fun at Death. "What, did you get lost on the way? Some king of the land you make."

Death ran away in a huff, and Tano claimed the hunter's friendship and his dinner. He also got to spend the night.

Now if this had been the end of it, Tano would have been the winner. And people would never have died.

But being a sneak, Death crept back while the hunter lay in bed. He took the only thing that Tano didn't claim: the hunter's sleep.

Even so, Death didn't get things all his own way. Thanks to Tano, Death couldn't claim the hunter's life until the man grew old.

This is why death sneaks up on people when they are least aware. This is also why death is sometimes called the "**eternal sleep.**"

---

[3] A compound is an enclosed living area that contains several dwellings.

INSIGHTS

Tano is one of the most important gods of the country of Togo in western Africa. He is a son of the Supreme God Nyamia. Tano is also honored as the creator of human beings. But he is perhaps best known as the god of the Tano River and the fertile lands through which it flows. However, Tano wasn't always ruler of this important river. Indeed, he had to trick his father to gain control of his river.

It seems that Nyamia thought that Tano was too disobedient to rule over the river. So the Supreme God was going to grant the river to his oldest son, Bia. He planned to give the barren and less fruitful places to Tano.

But Nyamia made the mistake of telling his plan to Goat, who was Tano's friend. Goat advised Tano to disguise himself as Bia and get to Nyamia's house early the next morning. Then Goat told Bia to take his time.

Tano did as Goat advised. Sure enough, Tano's disguise fooled his father. Without realizing it, Nyamia named Tano ruler of the fertile lands.

Bia angrily demanded his rights. But since Nyamia's word was law, it was too late to change his decision. Bia had to settle for second best.

"Death and the River King" explains why death sneaks up on people. But according to some African people, death doesn't always come as a surprise.

Some people of central Zaire believe that there are signs that a person is about to die. For example, a villager certainly wouldn't want to meet a young person with glowing eyes during a walk in the bush. This is a sign that the villager will die that night.

WALUMBE'S REVENGE

VOCABULARY PREVIEW

Below is a list of words that appear in the story. Read the list and get to know the words before you read the story.

commotion—fuss; noisy confusion
confront—challenge; stand up to
mortal—human being
outraged—offended; angry
possessive—controlling; selfish; stingy

Main Characters

Gulu—sky god
Kaizuki—oldest son of Gulu
Kintu—first man; husband of Nambi
Nambi—first woman; daughter of Gulu; wife of Kintu
Walumbe—son of Gulu

Walumbe, the youngest son of the sky god, was angry at his sister for marrying a human. But Walumbe found a way to get back at her. And his revenge is with us still.

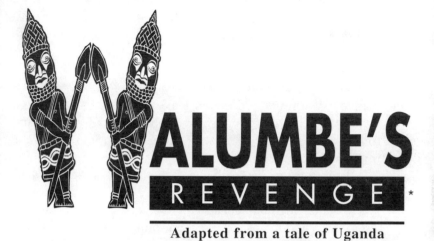

WALUMBE'S REVENGE *

Adapted from a tale of Uganda

This is how Death came to live here on earth.

Kintu[1]—the first man—and Nambi[2]—the first woman—got married in heaven. Nambi was the daughter of the sky god, Gulu.[3] He was happy for the couple. So was Nambi's brother, Kaizuki.[4] Both Gulu and Kaizuki attended the wedding and brought many gifts.

However, Walumbe[5]—Nambi's other brother—didn't attend the celebration.

---

* See "How Nambi Gained Her Beloved," pp. 3-9.
[1] (kin´ tu)
[2] (nam´ bē)
[3] (gu´ lu)
[4] (ka ē zu´ kē)
[5] (wal um´ bā)

He was very **possessive** of his royal sister and didn't want to let her go. He especially didn't want her to marry an ordinary **mortal** like Kintu. In fact, he had tried every trick he knew to prevent the wedding.

But despite Walumbe's tricks, Nambi became Kintu's bride. Then the couple prepared for the journey to earth. Nambi gathered her royal goats, sheep, and chickens while Kintu gathered his cows and his friend, the bee.

Before the couple left heaven, they went to say good-bye to Nambi's father. But as they prepared to go, Gulu gave the couple a warning. "Once you leave heaven, don't return," Gulu said sternly. "If you do, Walumbe will find you out and follow you to earth. There's no telling what tricks Walumbe might pull to get revenge."

Nambi thanked her father, and the couple started on their journey.

But after the couple had gone a short distance, Nambi's chickens began to fuss. They were hungry. However, being royalty, they refused to eat common seeds from the ground. They must have *royal* corn fed to them from their *royal* bowls. So they clucked, squawked, flapped their wings, and raised a **commotion** that could be heard for miles.

Such noise put Kintu and Nambi in great danger.

"Can't you keep your chickens quiet?" Kintu said. "Walumbe is sure to hear this noise and find us."

But Nambi's chickens continued to complain. Finally Nambi and Kintu decided to go back for the royal corn.

Gulu scolded the couple when he found that they had returned to heaven. "I told you not to ever come back here!" Gulu said with alarm. "Now Walumbe will surely find you."

Gulu hastily gave them the corn and told them to hurry away before Walumbe saw them.

The two left quickly. But just as Kintu and Nambi slipped out of heaven, Walumbe spied them. Unnoticed, he followed them to earth.

One day Walumbe appeared before the couple, hungry and tired of living alone. He asked his sister for some food.

Kintu was **outraged** when he saw Walumbe. "He isn't

welcome in our house," he told Nambi. "Keep him away from here."

Nambi tried her best to keep her brother away. But now that he knew where they lived, there was really nothing she could do.

As time passed, Nambi and Kintu became the parents of many children. Indeed, a comfortable village grew up around their house.

Of course, Walumbe was not allowed in the village. But when he saw how happy Kintu and Nambi were, he became jealous.

One day while Nambi was gone, Walumbe stood outside their house and called to Kintu. "I have no children to help me," Walumbe complained. "Could I borrow one or two of yours to help harvest my fields?"

"I've seen how you beat and starve your animals," Kintu told Walumbe. "I'll never even let you touch my children!"

"Unlike your chickens, your children aren't royalty," Walumbe shouted back. "Give me a child or you'll be sorry!"

"Never!"

The next morning Kintu's eldest son burned with fever. By sunset he was dead. Everybody grieved and wailed at the boy's funeral. Everybody but Walumbe, that is.

The next day another of Kintu's children fell ill and died, and then another.

Other children died. Then grown-ups began to die. Kintu believed that Walumbe was causing this sorrow. So he went to his father-in-law for help.

Gulu shook his head. "Remember how I warned you not to return to heaven? You and your people would have been protected against Walumbe and his deadly ways. But now he has followed you and knows where you live.

"I have only one suggestion," Gulu continued. "Maybe Nambi's older brother can do something to stop him. Kaizuki is the only one who ever stood up to Walumbe."

So Kintu went to Kaizuki with his problem. Kaizuki agreed to talk to Walumbe.

The next day Kaizuki appeared at Walumbe's door. "What good does it do to kill people?" Kaizuki asked his younger brother. "If you keep on killing, people will pay attention to you. But they won't serve you. And though they fear you, they'll never love you.

You're hurting them without gaining anything for yourself."

But Walumbe was angry and he was stubborn. He just kept on killing.

Kaizuki was afraid that death would claim more and more people until no one was left alive. But Walumbe still refused to listen to him. So Kaizuki was forced to **confront** Walumbe, and the two brothers fought.

Kaizuki was the stronger of the two, and he easily threw his brother to the ground. Walumbe quickly understood that he couldn't win in a fair fight. So he ran from his brother and disappeared into a hole near the town's goat pasture.

The villagers cheered when Kaizuki returned from the fight. But Kaizuki knew that Walumbe wasn't defeated. He told the townspeople to keep their children safely at home. Then he took a few brave men. They hid near the pasture and waited for Walumbe.

Meanwhile Walumbe got lonely hiding from everyone. So he sneaked out of his hole. He hoped that no one would notice him walking around.

Walumbe walked until he came to the goat pasture. But as he approached, the goats began bleating and making a terrible noise. For when Walumbe approached, they smelled Death.

Kaizuki heard the noise and rushed from his hiding place. But Walumbe saw him and disappeared again.

Walumbe made his home under the ground. He continued to hide and he continued to kill. Every so often, a child would die or an elder would not wake up. Everyone knew that Walumbe was at it again—he had taken more people to his underground home.

Kaizuki kept trying to find Walumbe to stop his killing. But Death—as Walumbe came to be called—always managed to escape. Finally Kaizuki got discouraged and returned to heaven.

Death, however, remains on earth, taking people back to his home whenever he gets lonely. He hasn't been captured yet.

INSIGHTS

This myth continues the Buganda story of the first man and woman. It is part of the epic of Kintu and Nambi. Because this epic has been told so many times, many versions of this myth exist. Sometimes Nambi is the one who returns for the corn. Sometimes it is Kintu who disobeys Gulu. But in all versions, Gulu tells the first people that because they returned to heaven, they have to die.

In "Walumbe's Revenge," people die because one of the first people made a mistake. The idea that people's foolishness caused death is common in other African stories as well.

In Zambia, the Ila say that the first man and woman were given a choice. The High God asked them to pick one of two bags. They selected the brighter sack, which contained death.

Feeling sorry for the couple, the creator gave them a second chance. If they were able to resist eating for a certain period of time, they would live forever. But the people ate before the time was up. The first man and woman never got another chance to live forever.

WHY FOLKS MUST DIE

VOCABULARY PREVIEW

Below is a list of words that appear in the story. Read the list and get to know the words before you read the story.

aggravated—angry
contemplate—think about carefully
fowl—bird
incompetent—unfit; unable
longevity—life span; length of life
malicious—cruel; mean
meddle—snoop; stick one's nose in
sneered—scoffed; talked down

Main Characters

Chameleon—messenger for the Supreme God
Monkey—messenger for the Supreme God
Unkulunkulu—Supreme God

WHY FOLKS MUST DIE

Inspired by a tale from the Zulu people

Chameleon was so proud to be chosen as the High God's messenger. Was it really his fault that people must die?

In the beginning, men and women lived for a very, very long time. In fact, they lived as long as trees. Now the Supreme God Unkulunkulu[1] approved of people living so long. In fact, he wanted to give them even greater **longevity.**

So Unkulunkulu decided to send the people a message. This message would let the people know that they would live forever.

"Send for Old Chameleon," Unkulunkulu told his servant. "Tell him that I

---

[1] (un´ ku lun´ ku lu)

have an important message that only he can carry."

The servant went in search of Old Chameleon. However, he learned that the lizard was out of town. So he sent for Old Chameleon's grandson instead.

Now chameleons are known for being smart. They are also known for being slow. But this particular chameleon, while extremely slow, was not very smart.

After several months, the young chameleon reached Unkulunkulu. The Great God was **aggravated** at the delay. "A man could grow old waiting for you to move from one place to another," he said angrily.

"Listen closely, Chameleon," Unkulunkulu continued in a stern voice. "You will be my messenger. Tell people that I have a gift for them. Tell them that people will never die and that they will live as long as gods. And Chameleon?"

"Yes, your majesty," replied the young lizard.

"You must hurry," ordered Unkulunkulu. "You have already let too much time go by."

The young chameleon's throat swelled with pride at this important task. He turned as red as the royal clay tile he sat upon. Then he crawled outside to **contemplate** this wonderful assignment.

Just as he stepped outside, Chameleon spied Monkey near the palace. "The Great Unkulunkulu has chosen me to give a message to the people," he bragged. "I take the place of my grandfather for this mission."

"Congratulations," Monkey said politely. "It's always good when our young folks can be of service to the Great God."

But after Chameleon left, Monkey went straight inside to complain to Unkulunkulu. "I happened to see a young chameleon leave your palace," he said to the Great God. "You thought his grandfather was slow? This one hasn't even gotten past the royal grounds. But maybe you're not in any hurry to tell folks anything.

"Not that it's any of my business," Monkey added as if he didn't care. "But I thought you ought to know."

Unkulunkulu was irritated to have Monkey **meddle** in his

business. But he was even more irritated to find that his servant had chosen an **incompetent** messenger.

"Then, Monkey, you shall take a message too. The message that reaches the people first will become the law. Tell folks that they are *not* like gods. They must die. In fact, people will not even live as long as trees."

Monkey rushed away with Unkulunkulu's message. As he left, he passed Chameleon. "See you around," **sneered** Monkey. "You can't crawl any faster than a yam can grow. And you're no smarter than a yam either."

Slow moving Chameleon thought about these **malicious** words for several days. Finally he decided to put them out of his mind. After all, he needed to concentrate on his duty. His grandfather would be very proud of the message he carried for Unkulunkulu.

Monkey, meanwhile, told everyone he saw—human, fish, and **fowl**—that they all must die. "And no, you're not like gods," Monkey said. "People won't even live as long as trees. Unkulunkulu told me this himself."

Several months later, Chameleon finally reached a group of men and women working in a field. Puffing himself up, he delivered his message. "The Great Unkulunkulu gives this gift to all people," he said. "All men and women will never die! Unkulunkulu says that people will live as long as gods. People will live even longer than trees."

But no one listened to Chameleon. In fact, they acted as if they didn't even hear him.

This wasn't the reaction he'd expected. Puzzled, Chameleon cleared his throat and repeated his message.

"Don't we wish," one of the people replied.

"What do you mean?" asked Chameleon.

"Monkey brought a message from the Great Unkulunkulu last spring," a man said. "Monkey told us that we must all die. We won't even live as long as trees."

Now this story tells two things. It tells why human beings die. And it tells that bad news, like gossip, travels faster than good.

INSIGHTS

This myth is from the Zulu people, whose homeland is in southern Africa. At one time, the Zulu nation was a warrior kingdom. In the 18th century, all young unmarried men had to serve in the Zulu army. A man couldn't even get married without the king's permission.

Today many of the two and a half million Zulus mine gold and diamonds.

As in "Why Folks Must Die," many African myths about death involve a problem with a message. Sometimes there are two different messengers. Sometimes there is one mixed-up message.

For example, some among the Nuer people say that the creator didn't know how long people would live. So he threw a piece of gourd into the water. If it floated, people would live forever. If it sank, people would have to die. The gourd floated!

God then sent a woman to share the good news with everyone else. The woman tried to show the people how God had made his decision. But she mistakenly threw a piece of a clay pot into the water. Of course, the heavy piece of pottery sank, so people had to die.

GODS AND MORTALS

The Poor-Minded Servant

How People Came to Be Different

The Man Who Argued with God

Most native African religions have one high god, with several lesser gods under him.

African mythology is full of people who don't understand the High God or who question his actions. Sometimes the people are punished for demanding too much of him. But other times the people are patiently taught the High God's point of view.

In either case, the people are given the opportunity to learn lessons that would help them live a better life.

THE POOR-MINDED SERVANT

VOCABULARY PREVIEW

Below is a list of words that appear in the story. Read the list and get to know the words before you read the story.

ancestors—ancient relatives; past family
invaluable—priceless; very valuable
favor—goodwill
mock—pretend; false
rebuking—scolding
timid—lacking courage

Main Characters

King of Kumasi—poor man's master
Nyambi—High God
Nyambi Ana— son of Nyambi
Poor man—servant of the King of Kumasi

THE

A poor man grew tired of being poor. So he complained to Nyambi, the Great God. Nyambi gave the man two chances to make his life better. But the man only proved that poor-minded people are poor for a reason.

OOR-MINDED
S E R V A N T

Adapted from an Ashanti legend

Now know the story of why certain folks who are poor will always stay that way.

There was once a poor man who farmed for the King of Kumasi.[1] He woke up poor, worked all day poor, and went to bed poor. His father and his father's father and his father's father's father were poor too.

Now there are many people who are poor. But this man would always complain about being poor. All his relatives before him had done the same thing.

Kumasi is the capital city of the Ashanti kingdom. It is located in Ghana.

"My life is wasted in the dust because of the God Nyambi,"[2] he would say. "Nyambi is the richest of the gods, yet he makes me suffer."

One day the man's words reached the ears of Nyambi. Concerned, Nyambi sent his son Nyambi Ana[3] down from the sky to bring the man back. Nyambi Ana did as he was asked and brought the man to his father's heavenly village. In this village lived **ancestors** of all the families on earth.

"I'm told," said Nyambi, "that you fuss about being poor. Since you are so unhappy, I'll let you change families. Pick out the family that you would rather be part of. See if that makes things better for you. But remember, it is not I who causes your suffering."

The man carefully studied all the families. There were so many! He could choose to be part of a very rich family. He could choose to be part of a family that was very poor. Or he could choose any other in-between stage of family life.

But the man was **timid** at heart and afraid of trying new things. So when he saw his own family, he immediately selected it.

Nyambi nodded. "As you know, your family has never enjoyed material wealth. There are no riches there now, and there never will be. Yet that is the family that you have chosen to return to."

Nyambi paused and studied the man. Then he said, "I will go even further for you. I will give you the chance to change your condition and your future. I shall give you a gift."

As the man watched with hungry eyes, Nyambi produced two sacks: one tiny and one huge. "One is for you," Nyambi said. "The other you must give to your master—the King of Kumasi. You must choose wisely. I will not tell which you should keep for yourself and which you should give to the king."

After begging his leave from Nyambi, the poor man took both sacks and returned to earth. But before he presented him-

[2] (nē yam´ bē)
[3] (nē yam´ bē a´ na)

self to the king, he hid the big sack in a field hog's burrow. He had to act quickly, for he didn't want to be seen. Even though he didn't look into the bags, he was sure that the large sack was full of gold or some other **invaluable** substance.

Then the poor man prepared himself to meet his master. He was very nervous. He was afraid the king would be angry with him for being away from the fields.

The man met with a surprise. Instead of **rebuking** him for his absence, the king asked about his trip. "So you have been to visit Nyambi," the king said with **mock** interest. "Tell me, does the Supreme Ruler have a message for me?"

"The God Nyambi gives you this gift," the man said.

The king smiled. "How kind it was of Nyambi to think of me." He figured the sack was actually from the man to get back into his **favor.**

But when the king opened the little sack, he let out a cry of wonder. Inside he found gold dust worth a fortune. At once he realized that the gift could not have been from his servant.

Horrified, the poor man rushed away to the field hog's hole. With shaking hands, he reached for the big sack. But when he opened it, he found only stones.

Then the voice of Nyambi spoke to him. "To be poor is not a crime. To be poor-minded is. The child of poor-minded parents never becomes rich. If he gains some wealth, it slips through his fingers. Poor-minded you are, and poor you will always be."

INSIGHTS

The word "Ashanti" can describe a people, a language, or a kingdom. The great kingdom the Ashanti people once ruled is now the country of Ghana in western Africa.

In Ashanti tradition, stools are more than just seats—they're also homes for the souls of the dead.

The Ashanti believe that when a person dies, the soul of the dead person continues to live in that person's personal stool. Families often have a special "stool house" where they keep the stools of their ancestors.

The Ashanti also have a stool for their entire nation. The story of this stool is told in a legend.

In the 18th century, a neighboring kingdom tried to conquer the Ashanti. A medicine man named Anochi prayed to the High God for help. In answer, a Golden Stool came down from the sky. Anochi told the people that the stool held the soul of the nation. United by the Golden Stool, the Ashanti overthrew their enemy.

The Golden Stool is still kept in the royal palace at Kumasi. Some believe that if the stool is ever stolen, great harm will come to the Ashanti.

The Ashanti are also famous for their "talking drums." In many African languages, the meaning of a word often depends on its pitch. So drums can "talk" by imitating the pitches of words.

A drum message can be heard up to seven miles away. If the message is important, those who hear it will send it on to the next village. Eventually the message gets to the right person because everyone has a special drum name.

HOW PEOPLE CAME TO BE DIFFERENT

VOCABULARY PREVIEW

Below is a list of words that appear in the story. Read the list and get to know the words before you read the story.

discord—argument; conflict
distracted—confused; bothered
obsessed—caught up in; excited
predict—tell the future; forecast
recounted—repeated
unique—different; one of a kind
vices—moral weaknesses; bad habits

Main Characters

Chameleon—messenger for Olorun
Great Thinker—man full of ideas
Obatala—god who created humans
Olorun—High God

*The first people had everything
they needed. But they weren't
satisfied and asked for more.
These foolish people forgot how
dangerous it can be to get exactly
what you ask for.*

How People Came to Be

DiFFeReNT

Inspired by a Yoruba tale

In the Yoruba city of Ife[1] the
High God Olorun[2] kept all the
people happy. No one had less
than another. No one had
more than another. Everyone
had the same color of hair,
eyes, and skin. Life was good.

Oh, there were a few peo-
ple who were shaped differently, but no one really
noticed. This happened
because Obatala[3] was drunk
with palm wine when he created the first people. You see,

---

[1] (ē´fay) Ife is a city in western Nigeria.
[2] (ōl´ ōr un) Olorun is the Supreme God of the Yoruba people.
[3] (ōb a tal´ a) Obatala is the creator of humans. (See "Obatala Creates the World,"
pp. 11-17.)

he dropped a few on the ground by mistake. The person who fell on his head was called the Great Thinker.

This one thought long, long, long thoughts and made long, long, long speeches. People usually would nod politely at him and go on about their business.

One day the Great Thinker finished a particularly long thought. Then he began an equally long speech. "Why must we all be the same color?" he asked. "Why is it that no one has more or less than another? Isn't this way of life boring to you?"

People had begun to gather around, so the thinker spoke on. "Olorun answers each of our needs the same way. Wouldn't you like to be **unique?** Wouldn't you like to have things no one else has?"

The thinker became **obsessed** with this thought. The more people listened, the more he carried on and on about it. Finally others began to agree with him.

"It would be nice to have a house that doesn't look the same as everybody else's," said one man. "Often I've gone into my neighbor's home by mistake."

"Obatala gives every family a firstborn at the same time," said a woman. "When we hold our naming ceremonies, everybody else does too. Then we give our children the same name. It would be better to hold individual ceremonies and give our children different names."

That's how it began. More and more people began to grumble and complain about the sameness of everything. They began to argue with each other too. When people argued, the noise attracted quite a crowd. No one had ever argued in Ife before. Soon after the arguments started, gossip appeared among the people. Soon came greed and other **vices.**

The **discord** became so loud that it reached Olorun's ears. Of course, being the Supreme Ruler, he hesitated to visit Ife himself. Instead, he sent his special messenger, Chameleon, to find out what the problem was.

However, Chameleon was a rather slow messenger. You see, he was easily **distracted.** With each eye, separately, he looked at every single thing along his path. With each ear, separately, he listened to every single noise. Needless to say, when he reached Ife, he got both eyes and both ears full.

"Give me this! Give me that! More cloth! More palm nuts! More hoes! More gold, silver, drums, goats, children, wives, seeds, houses, jewelry! More, more, more—but just for me!"

The people of Ife wanted different colors of hair and different shades of skin. Some thought lighter skin was prettier. Others thought darker skin was better. People even asked for different colors of rain to fall upon their crops.

"Great Olorun, it's a mess," Chameleon said when he returned. He **recounted** for Olorun every single desire that every single person of Ife had expressed. Three days later, he finished listing the requests of the people of Ife.

"I will grant their every wish right now," Olorun said. "But I **predict** that they will not be happy anymore. In a year's time, go back down and see how they're doing."

A year later Chameleon returned to Ife. He found the people in an uproar. Their desires had all been met, but this had only made things worse.

Chameleon first stopped before a small group of men and women. "The Great Olorun sends this message," he began. "Your wishes have been granted. But—"

"And it's all your fault!" a woman interrupted angrily. "You should have told Olorun to give me what I wanted *after* my neighbor received her wishes. I asked for two goats, five pieces of gold, and red hair. My neighbor saw my gifts and asked for *three* goats, *ten* pieces of gold, and *blonde* hair. And now she has more. She brags! Such nerve!"

The women and men began to argue among themselves. They even threw rocks at each other. Poor Chameleon crawled into a grove of palm trees and watched from there. He sent up a prayer for help to Olorun.

"Enough is enough," said Olorun when he heard Chameleon's prayer. "The people want to be different! We'll give them just what they want!"

In the twinkle of an eye, Olorun gave the arguing people different languages. From that day forward, the people could not understand one another. Then Olorun scattered the people to all corners of the land.

Since that time, people have realized their mistake. Every so often, people try to understand each other and overcome their differences. But after a short time, greed, gossip, and misunderstandings rise up again. So it has been ever since the Great Thinker thought his foolish thoughts.

INSIGHTS

The chameleon is an important animal in African mythology. Stories about this creature are found all over the continent.

In many myths, the chameleon delivers the High God's messages to humans. However, in Zaire the chameleon itself is considered a god. And in the Congo, the Pygmies pray to the chameleon when they need rain.

Africans respect the chameleon because it moves cautiously and silently. Thus it symbolizes wisdom. Some peoples even claim to be descended from the wise chameleon.

"How People Came to Be Different" briefly mentions Yoruba naming ceremonies. For some Yoruba parents, choosing a baby's name is not a task to be taken lightly. The fact that the names chosen are often similar to those of the gods proves how important naming is.

The day the naming ceremony is held depends on the sex of the child. If the baby is a girl, she is named on the seventh day after birth. If the baby is a boy, he is named on the ninth day after birth. Because twins are special to the Yoruba, the eighth day after birth is set aside just for their naming.

The Yoruba are not the only African people to have a story about people wanting too much. The Basotho of southern Africa tell about a young prince who demanded that the King give him the moon. His foolish father gave in to the prince's demand and promised to get it for him. The King had a great tower built that reached all the way to the sky. But the man who tried to bring down the moon poked a hole in it, causing a great explosion. The King, the prince, and all the people were killed.

The moon still shines in the heavens, but the greedy people and their entire country were destroyed.

THE MAN WHO ARGUED WITH GOD

VOCABULARY PREVIEW

Below is a list of words that appear in the story. Read the list and get to know the words before you read the story.

astonishment—great surprise; amazement
brooded—sulked; grieved
mourning—grief; sadness caused by death of a loved one
pleas—requests; appeals
radiated—shone in all directions
serenity—calm; peace of mind
vanity—self-love

Main Characters

Chagga man
Great One—High God
Wife of Chagga man

"All that God does is good,"
says an African proverb. But a
father whose children died
didn't believe it. The grieving
man vowed to kill God. Here is
what happened when he met
God face-to-face.

The Man

Who Argued with God

Inspired by a tale from the Chagga people of Kenya

In the Chagga[1] kingdom there lived a man and a woman who had ten fine children—five sons and five daughters. But these children all died and went to heaven to be with God. They left their father and mother behind.

The man became very angry with God for having taken his children. He endlessly **brooded** over this tragic event. His wife was in **mourning** too. But she accepted the will of God. She begged her husband to keep the faith, for God knew best.

[1] The homeland of the Chagga people is on the border between Kenya and Tanzania.

But the man cursed God to his friends and enemies alike. His friends offered prayers. His enemies offered revenge.

"Kill God," his enemies said. "Go to the spearmaker for ten sharp spears. Use them to kill the one who killed your children—especially your sons."

The foolish man did as his enemies said. Ignoring the **pleas** of his wife, he set out to find the place where God lived. He carried ten sharp spears to kill God with—one spear for each dead child.

The man walked and he walked through many lands. In each village he asked where God lived. Nobody knew.

Finally he stopped an old man. "Where does God live?" he asked. "I seek revenge from him for taking my children."

"Be blessed it was God and not the devil who took your children," the old man replied. "Be blessed that you even had sons and daughters. All things work for good when God is involved. Let your anger pass and praise God for his wisdom. You will be rewarded for your faith."

"You're no help," the angry man said and continued his search for God.

Finally the man came to an ocean. There he found crowds of people lining the shores. The people buzzed and hummed with excitement. As the man watched, a griot[2] passed by and strode out upon the beach. "Make way for the King of all Men!" the griot shouted.

Then in the center of the crowd, a tall Black man appeared. Around him a golden light **radiated**.

The angry man quickly hid in a grove of palm trees.

Cries rose and fell like the waves of the sea. "All praise to the Great One!" the people shouted. The Black man smiled upon the crowd. Then, to the **astonishment** of the man, the Great One walked straight to the palm trees where he had hidden. The Great One spread wide his arms.

"Welcome, my son. You're the man who holds such sorrow and anger against me."

The man said nothing.

---

[2] (grē′ ō) A griot is a historian and storyteller of western Africa who performs community histories.

"Yes, your children are now with me," the Great One said. "If you still wish to get revenge by spearing me, I am here. But before you do, please see your sons and daughters."

The Great One motioned to ten young people standing in the crowd. They came forward and embraced their father. The man then saw that his children were the same and yet not the same.

On earth their faces had held expressions of pride, **vanity,** greed, anger, ignorance, and other traits of human weakness. But now the father saw that their faces shone with **serenity** and happiness.

The words of the old man came back to the Chagga man. He realized that the Great One's will was best. He dropped his spears to the ground. "My children belong to you," the man said. "My faith was weak. Please forgive me."

"That you seek forgiveness shows your faith is still strong," the Great One said. "Return to your wife and remember your blessings and your faith. With faith comes riches."

The man returned home to his loyal wife and vowed to renew his faith. He planted his crops and tended them without complaint. He sang the praises of God to all who would listen. He learned not to listen to his enemies.

After a year his wife announced that she was with child, and they rejoiced when she gave birth to a son. In time more sons and daughters were born to them. Because of their faith, the Chagga man and his wife grew rich beyond their imaginations.

INSIGHTS

The homeland of the Chagga people is in Kenya, a country on the east coast of Africa. Most of the Chagga live in the highlands, where they farm the rich soil.

These people have a unique farming custom. What they grow depends on whether they are male or female.

For instance, only the women grow beans, sweet potatoes, and yams. And only men grow bananas. Both men and women grow corn.

The Chagga speak one of the many Bantu languages. The first Bantu speakers lived in the Congo River basin in west central Africa. From there, they moved to eastern and southern Africa.

This migration began over 2,000 years ago, during the Iron Age. At first, the Bantu moved east, to the Great Lakes region. But that area became crowded, so some tribes moved south. By 300 A.D., the Bantu had spread to what is now South Africa. Today, more than two-thirds of all Africans are descended from these Bantu migrants.

As they traveled, the Bantu taught other people to raise cattle and use iron farm tools. They also spread their language. Today over 500 variations of the Bantu language are spoken in central and southern Africa.

Most Bantu languages are genderless. That is, they do not have words like "he" and "she." Only a person's name indicates whether that person is male or female.

Bantu homesteads generally don't have a large family house. Instead, many separate huts serve specific functions. One hut is for unmarried boys; another is for single girls. Then there is a separate hut for each wife and her children. Another hut serves as a kitchen and still another as a food storage hut.

TRICKSTERS

Tortoise Cracks His Shell

Brother Spider Gets Stuck

Hare Causes Big Trouble

Tricksters are found in myths all over the world. They are often small animals who cause big trouble.

Africans tell stories about several different tricksters. Three of the most popular tricksters are Tortoise, Spider, and Hare. Each of these tricksters is something like the animal he's named after. But each has some human and supernatural qualities too. In fact, some groups honor the trickster as a god.

Trickster myths are often humorous. Even when tricksters get into trouble, there's no cause to worry. They just bounce back and start more trickery.

TORTOISE CRACKS HIS SHELL

VOCABULARY PREVIEW

Below is a list of words that appear in the story. Read the list and get to know the words before you read the story.

buff—polish
compliment—praise
concern—business
discarded—thrown away
glossy—bright and shiny
sported—showed off
valet—servant

Main Characters

Buzzard—friend of Monkey and Tortoise
Monkey—Tortoise's friend and servant
Tortoise—trickster

Tortoise usually got what he wanted. But sometimes his lack of self-control landed him in trouble. In this story, Tortoise's pride causes his fall.

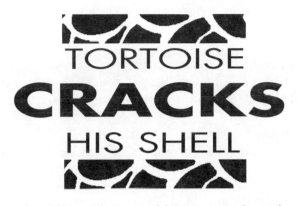

TORTOISE CRACKS HIS SHELL

Inspired by numerous African tortoise tales

Don't let Tortoise's version of how his shell was broken stir your sympathy. It's his own fault—and no one else's—that his shell is cracked. Monkey, who was Tortoise's personal **valet,** knows the whole story.

Tortoise once **sported** a brilliant yellow undershell. It was as smooth and shiny as an elephant's tusk. Everybody said Tortoise's shell was the most beautiful thing around.

Well, his friends—Monkey and Buzzard—*told* Tortoise everybody said so. Tortoise got quite vain over such praise— particularly the praise of Monkey. So he hired Monkey to wax his undershell with palm oil. Monkey would **buff** the shell with Buzzard's **discarded** feathers. Then he would polish Tortoise's toenails with red berry juice.

Monkey kept Tortoise right side up too. (He did that for free.)

One day Buzzard suggested that Tortoise lie on his back and have a special weekend showing. "The way you sit now, the animals can only see the top of your shell. If you turn over, even the goats high on the mountains will see your undershell."

Tortoise thought that was a great idea.

"I'm not so sure," Monkey told Tortoise when they were alone. "I saw Buzzard lick his lips when he made that suggestion. All he ever thinks about is his next meal. If you turned over, you'd dry up and die. Next thing you know, you'd be breakfast for Old Baldbrain. You stick with me and you won't go wrong."

One day Monkey was waxing, buffing, polishing, and praising Tortoise. "Your shell is almost as bright as the sun himself," Monkey told him.

This, indeed, was the highest **compliment** Tortoise had ever heard. "Pour a little more oil on me, right in the middle where my wide spots are."

"And, Tortoise, the sun couldn't hold a candle to you. You're so bright you could make crops grow—I bet you could even dry up lakes."

"Really?" Tortoise blushed and began to think great thoughts. "I could make grass grow and make water disappear? That's big time!"

Monkey began to sing. He used up half a bottle of oil and fifteen buzzard feathers listening to himself.

> You could hang up there in the sky all day.
> Knock that old sun out of the way.
> Bright all day and bright all night.
> Either way you go, you'd be dynamite!

All afternoon Tortoise thought about himself and the sun. He decided that Monkey was right. He looked around until he saw Buzzard in a tree not far away.

"Buzzard, do you think my shell is shiny?" Tortoise asked.

"Just thinking how **glossy** it is myself," said Buzzard. Actually Buzzard had been listening to his own stomach growl.

"Is it really as bright as the sun?"

"Just as bright, if not brighter."

Tortoise got so excited he began to pant. "So bright it could grow crops and dry up lakes?" he cried. "That's what Monkey told me. He said I should hang up in the sky all day and knock the old sun out of the way."

"Well, why not?" said Buzzard, who never believed a word Monkey said.

"Then that settles it. Buzzard, will you take me up into the sky? I want to start raising crops and drying up lakes."

"Be happy to," said Buzzard. He didn't ask how Tortoise was planning to *stay* in the sky. That wasn't his **concern.**

Tortoise clumsily pulled himself onto Buzzard's back. Buzzard lifted his wings and carried Tortoise into the air. Soon the two animals were soaring high over the land.

Tortoise was excited. He imagined himself making the corn grow and causing the yams to sprout. He pictured the animals' surprise when he rose in the east the next morning.

Tortoise couldn't wait any longer. He waved his paw in the air. "This spot looks good. Just let me off right here."

"Okay, here you go," Buzzard said as he shook Tortoise off his back.

However, Tortoise didn't hang in the sky. He fell straight to the ground and bounced three times.

When Tortoise regained consciousness, he was thankful to see that he was still in one piece. But his shell wasn't. Pieces were scattered all over the ground. Monkey was picking them up and putting them in a basket.

"You and Old Baldbrain sure get some great ideas," Monkey said with disgust.

Tortoise hurt too much to answer. For a small fee, Monkey patched Tortoise's shell back together. He didn't do a very good job, though.

Now whenever anyone comes near, Tortoise pulls his head inside his shell. He's ashamed of his cracked shell and his vanity that led to his fall.

INSIGHTS

Africans have many stories about Tortoise. They admire his ability to survive. There is a Swahili song about his tough shell: "I move house and yet I never move house. I'm at home wherever I travel."

Tortoise is protected by his wits as well as his shell. For example, in one myth Tortoise was caught by a lion. Tortoise reminded Lion that his shell was too tough to chew. But if Lion just put him in the river, his shell would soften. The hungry lion threw Tortoise into the water, and the trickster escaped.

In another tale Tortoise used his quick wits to win a race with Hare. Tortoise asked members of his family to line up all along the racetrack. Hare ran as fast as he could, but a tortoise always appeared ahead of him.

The Yoruba call the Tortoise *Ijapa*. They have many proverbs about this trickster. Some of these wise sayings are about ways people should be like Ijapa. For example, "It is a cautious person like a tortoise who can see a tortoise in the bush." This means that if you stay alert, you won't be tricked.

However, other proverbs show the Tortoise acting in ways people should never behave. For example, Ijapa once went to a feast with his son hidden in his pocket. Every time the Tortoise put a bite of food in his mouth, he put another in his pocket. However, his trick was discovered. Ever since, saying that someone gives "one morsel to the mouth, one to the pocket" means that person is dishonest.

BROTHER SPIDER GETS STUCK

VOCABULARY PREVIEW

Below is a list of words that appear in the story. Read the list and get to know the words before you read the story.

ambled—strolled; walked slowly
arrogance—disregard; disrespect
desperation—despair; sorrow
hearty—warm; cheerful
hobbled—limped; walked lamely
reputation—a person's status or character as seen by others
reserve—supply; stock

Main Characters

Brother Spider—trickster; husband of Sister Spider
Sister Spider—wife of Brother Spider

Africans say, "The wisdom of the spider is greater than that of all the world put together." But one time Spider was too clever for his own good. In this story, the trickster is finally tricked.

Brother Spider Gets Stuck

Inspired by a Hausa tale

Sister Spider and her husband Brother Spider were ordinary spiders of the garden variety. Of course, garden spiders are famous for being excellent farmers. But Brother Spider preferred to think instead of farm. No, he wasn't lazy. One cannot be lazy and also think, because thinking takes work.

The rest of the villagers were garden spiders too. They spent all their time farming and talking about farming. They also gossiped about Sister Spider's husband.

Don't get me wrong. They appreciated thinking and thinkers. But they didn't appreciate Brother Spider's way of thinking, which usually involved a good deal of palm wine and long naps. His kind of thinking didn't put food on the table.

Come each spring, everybody else tilled the soil, planted seeds, and weeded their crops. Sister Spider, who had arthritis[1] in all her legs, did what she could. Come each fall, everybody else harvested crops. Sister Spider, who also had a bad back, harvested the few crops she had. Come each winter, everybody else had food. But Sister Spider usually had to beg food from her daughter-in-law.

Sister Spider had also tried weaving cloth and exchanging it for food in the market. But now her arthritis kept her from such work.

This particular spring, Sister Spider was mighty worried. She didn't know how she could get the crop planted.

Sister Spider turned to her husband. She found him lying on a grass mat, eating beans. As usual, he was thinking.

"Can you help me with the planting today?" she asked.

"Tomorrow for sure," Brother Spider replied. "Do we have seeds?"

Sister Spider frowned. "I thought we had seeds from our daughter-in-law's old crop."

Brother Spider stopped chewing. "Oh no, they shriveled up long ago. Without seeds, we can't plant our crops. Let me think about that."

Sister Spider was old, but she wasn't a fool. You don't get to be old being a fool. She knew that the very beans Brother Spider was eating were the last of their tiny **reserve** of seeds.

Sister Spider sighed. Once again, she went on over to her daughter-in-law's home and begged eight handfuls of seeds from her.

---

[1] Arthritis causes the joints of the body to swell and become painful.

The next morning Sister Spider cornered her husband. "We now have seeds," she said. "Can you help prepare the ground?"

"I would gladly have turned over the ground long ago," Brother Spider said. "But you didn't get the hoe sharpened, remember? Let me think about how we can get that done."

What Sister Spider remembered was that Brother Spider had lost the hoe last fall. So she again went to her daughter-in-law's home and borrowed an old rusty hoe. Then she patiently scraped the blade against a rock until it was sharp.

The next morning Sister Spider gave her husband the hoe and the seeds. With a shrug of his shoulders, Brother Spider went off to the fields. Every day that summer he went to the fields. Meanwhile, Sister Spider repaired her loom and tried her hand at weaving cloth again.

When harvest time arrived, Sister Spider saw everybody else bring home food. But Brother Spider brought home no food.

Curious and hungry, Sister Spider decided to visit Brother Spider in the field. She found him on his grass mat. His legs were crossed one upon the other, upon the other, upon the other. And upon the other and the other and the other and the other. He was eating dried yams and drinking palm wine. Sister Spider frowned when she saw him get up and hide his refreshments in a hole and cover it over.

"That lazy Brother Spider! I should have known!" said Sister Spider as she **hobbled** back home. She was as mad as her cousin the hornet. "I'll fix him," she said to herself.

Back home, she cut out the figure of a female spider from a strip of bark. Then she carefully smeared the figure with sticky fruit gum. With a glint in her eye, she took the figure back to the field. This time, she found Brother Spider asleep on the ground.

Quietly she set the figure on top of the covered hole where Brother Spider had put his palm wine. Then she hid.

Presently Brother Spider woke up. "I must have a quick snack before I go home to Ol' Grumble Lips," he said aloud.

Grumble Lips! Sister Spider almost came out from her

hiding spot.

Just then Brother Spider saw the figure at his hiding place. "Ho! And who are you? A thief! Be gone!" he roared.

Brother Spider looked again. "Oh, a lady!" he murmured.

Pulling up his stomach, Brother Spider **ambled** over to the figure. In a **hearty** voice, he bid her hello.

The figure, of course, said nothing. Angered by her **arrogance,** Brother Spider lifted one of his arms. "Playing hard to get, Miss Uppity? Speak up, or else I'll bounce you a couple on both sides of your face!"

The creature stayed quiet.

"Warned you! Here I go!"

Spider smacked the creature—Blam! Blam!—on the left side of its head. Then Spider smacked it—Blip! Blip!—on the right side. Brother Spider tried to pull back, but to his horror, he found two of his arms stuck fast to the sticky girl's head.

"Let go! I'm a married man!" Brother Spider shouted. "Telling you, woman, to cut me loose, or I'll kick you in the knees! No? Well then, take this and this and this and this!"

Brother Spider kicked the spider girl—Bop! Bop!—in her left knees and then—Bap! Bap!—in her right. Of course, his legs stuck fast.

Sister Spider, watching from behind a tree, couldn't help chuckling at the sight. Then she began to laugh. She laughed so hard she fell back on the ground. She threw all her arms over her mouth to hold in the sound. Then she sat up and peeped out again.

"Humph! Let me go, I said!" Brother Spider shouted. "My wife'll be coming along any minute. I'll tell her you ate our crops. You'll be in deep trouble when she gets here!"

Brother Spider jerked and pulled, but he couldn't get loose. Finally, in **desperation,** he hit the fruit gum girl with his head. Of course, all of Brother Spider was stuck to the creature now.

Sister Spider laughed so hard she had to hang on to the tree. Then she sat down and peeped out again.

"Oh, please let me go," Brother Spider begged the fruit gum girl. "I'll never say a word about this to anybody. Now just let me loose before the other folks leave their fields and see us like this. You know, it won't be good for your **reputation.** And I'll never live it down that I got beat up by some ol' sticky fruit gum girl."

Of course, that didn't work. Presently Brother Spider began to hear voices in the distance. The other folks were beginning to leave their fields.

Brother Spider began to cry. "Oh please, Miss Sticky Lady, let me loose. I let Sister Spider think I've been raising crops out here, but I haven't planted a thing. I admit that I haven't done my duty. But if you let me go, I'll change my ways!"

At these pitiful words, Sister Spider felt sorry for her husband. She sent up a prayer to the rain god. She asked him to wash Brother Spider loose from the sticky woman. Then she started back home. Just as she was about to enter the house, it began to rain.

Before long, Brother Spider came home. He sheepishly slipped in, sopping wet and smelling like fruit.

"You know, I've been thinking. I think I'll give up farming. And while I'm at it, I may as well give up palm wine too. I'd much rather help you right here at home. I think I'll try something new."

Brother Spider pulled Sister Spider's old loom into their house and set it in the corner. He figured out how to weave in record time. He got so good at it, all the other spiders learned how to weave too. They've been doing it ever since, especially in the corners of people's homes.

80

INSIGHTS

The African spider trickster is often called *Anansi*. In most tales about Anansi, he manages to outsmart his rivals. Indeed, Spider is so cunning that he sometimes acts as the High God's chief official.

But on occasion, Spider's tricks backfire. That's when he becomes the object of his own jokes. However, don't let that fool you. Anansi is still a trickster. One African proverb warns, "Woe to him who would put his trust in Anansi—a sly, selfish, and greedy fellow."

Tales about Spider are common throughout Africa. The story presented here is told among the Hausa people near Nigeria.

The Hausa were originally organized in seven independent city-states. In the 1500s, Muslim traders from northern Africa began winning converts to Islam. Today the majority of the estimated nine million Hausa are Muslims.

Stories about Spider are also told in America. Here Anansi is often called Nansi or Annancy.

The most popular story that parallels "Brother Spider Gets Stuck" is "The Tar Baby." It is one of the most popular stories in African-American folklore.

HARE CAUSES BIG TROUBLE

VOCABULARY PREVIEW

Below is a list of words that appear in the story. Read the list and get to know the words before you read the story.

complement—go together; balance
distinguished—dignified; elegant
nuisance—bother; pest
privately—secretly; individually
snubbed—insulted; put off
statuesque—huge; great; impressive

Main Characters

Hare—trickster
Hippo—friend of Rhino
Rhino—friend of Hippo

Hippo and Rhino were the best of friends. But to these two colossal animals, the Hare was just a small nuisance. With rumors and gossip, Hare found a way to get noticed.

Hare Causes Big Trouble

INSPIRED BY A SWAHILI TALE

It is said that Hippo and Rhino were once best friends. They thought of each other as **statuesque** in size and **distinguished** in looks. They shared the same tick bird[1] to rid them of bugs. They drank from the same watering hole. They even slept in each other's wallows.[2]

Now Hare was jealous of the larger animals' friendship. Hare talked about the two animals behind their backs. He said they were fat, greedy, loud, and ugly.

But Hare was all smiles to their faces. "Oh, you two have so much in common," he would say. "You **complement** each other."

While Hare made fun of the two large animals, he secretly wished that he could share their

---

[1] A tick bird eats insects that live on large animals.
[2] Wallows are mud holes that animals roll around in.

friendship. But every time he tried to make friends, he made a **nuisance** of himself. He danced on their heads when they lay in their wallows. He splashed in their drinking hole and muddied up the water.

All of this got their attention, but not their friendship.

One day Rhino and Hippo grew tired of Hare's silly behavior.

"Hippo, do you feel a flea?" asked Rhino when Hare hopped on Hippo's back.

"Either a flea or a fly," said Hippo as he rolled over on his back. The surprised Hare was nearly smashed by the large Hippo.

Well, Hare didn't take kindly to being called names. For days, he was angry at the way the two animals **snubbed** him. Finally Hare decided he must stand up for his honor. "If I can't enjoy the friendship of Hippo and Rhino," Hare said to himself, "then neither shall they!" He immediately got to work on a plan.

First he made a long rope from thick vines growing in the forest. Then he went to Rhino at the water hole.

"Hippo told me he's ten times stronger than you," Hare said slyly.

"That may be," Rhino laughed.

"He said you were ugly too," Hare went on.

Rhino suddenly remembered something. Hippo *had* said words to that effect many years ago—before they had become such good friends. It had made Rhino mad then, and it began to make him mad all over again.

"Tell me what else that ugly thing said," Rhino demanded.

"I don't know what Hippo had in mind," Hare continued innocently, "but he sent me to you with this rope. He said something about pulling you out of your sorry mud hole."

"Sorry mud hole, huh?" said Rhino, his voice rising. "You can tell him for me that I would be doing him a favor if I pulled him from that pig sty he lives in. Tie your rope to my back leg. Tell Hippo to prepare to find another home."

Hare took the other end of the rope and went in search of the other large animal. He found Hippo lying in his favorite wallow.

"Hippo," whispered Hare, "Rhino has been talking behind your back. He says you're weak and that your wallow smells like a pig sty."

"How's that?" said Hippo, who was a bit deaf.

Hare repeated his words. "He said he was tired of visiting your lousy mud hole. He says you're fat too." Hare held up the rope. "He challenges you to a tug of war."

Hippo thought this was strange talk to come from his friend of many years. But he remembered something mean Rhino had once said about him—something about how fat he was.

Hippo felt pride rise up inside his huge chest. "Tie that rope!" he roared.

Hare quickly tied the rope around Hippo's back left leg. "I'll tell you when to pull," Hare said. "By the way, Rhino also said you were ugly."

Hippo became enraged. He *knew* that he was much handsomer than Rhino ever could be. He charged off on his thick, short legs, pulling the rope tight. Rhino, feeling the tug, thundered away in the opposite direction.

Hare watched from a small hill. He laughed to see the two friends fighting against each other.

Hippo pulled and strained. "Say I'm fat?" he roared. "I'll show you!"

Rhino dug his feet into the ground and pulled hard too. "Think I'm ugly, do you? I'll show you!"

The rope, being only made of vines, popped. With a tremendous roar, both Hippo and Rhino fell over on their faces.

Hare gave out a shriek of laughter, lost his balance, and rolled right down the hill. He rolled first past Rhino, who got to his feet and gave chase. Then he rolled past Hippo, who prepared to follow. The two friends then came face to face.

"So I'm ugly, am I?" Rhino pawed the ground and shook his horn for battle.

"Well, you called me fat," shouted Hippo.

"I did no such thing," Rhino said back. "Hare told me

what you said."

Rhino stopped shouting. So did Hippo. They both turned to Hare, who ran off laughing.

Since that time, Hippo and Rhino have had only a polite friendship. They meet only at the watering hole—one on each side.

Jealousy—for that is Hare's real name—drinks there too. And he still whispers **privately** to each former friend about the other.

INSIGHTS

This story about the hare is from the Swahili culture. No one group can be called "Swahili." Swahili is a language spoken by many groups in eastern Africa. This language combines Bantu and Arabic.

In another version of this story, Hare tricks Elephant and Hippo into a tug of war. The larger animals get so angry at Hare for causing trouble that they won't let him eat grass or drink water. But Hare tricks them a second time. He claims to have a terrible illness that others can catch. So Elephant and Hippo run away before they get sick. Meanwhile, Hare stays behind and stuffs himself on grass and water.

The tug-of-war theme is so popular in Africa that there is even a dilemma story about it. This type of story ends with a question for the audience to answer.

In the dilemma story, Elephant and Hippo don't realize they've been tricked. They even admit that Hare is their equal. Then they let Hare sit with them in the highest places in the animal council. The question is: Are these animals really equal?

HOW AND WHY

How Lightning Came to Be

Why Mosses and Vines Grow on Trees

Why the Bat Sleeps Upside Down

How is lightning created? What causes people to fall in love? Why do bats sleep in caves?

Humans have asked questions like these since the beginning of time. And people have often looked to mythology for answers.

The three how and why myths in this section not only provide some interesting explanations. They also reveal the humor and wisdom of the African people who tell the stories.

HOW LIGHTNING CAME TO BE

VOCABULARY PREVIEW

Below is a list of words that appear in the story. Read the list and get to know the words before you read the story.

berserk—crazy; wild
distressed—alarmed; worried
empathy—understanding; concern
gnash—strike together; grind
roused—excited; stirred
suppress—hide; hold back

Main Characters

King—ruler of villagers and animals
Mother Sheep—mother of Ram
Ram—Mother Sheep's son

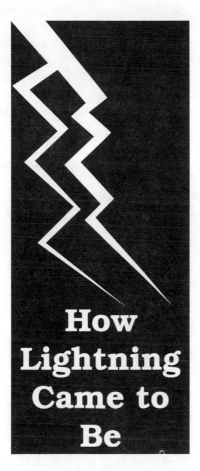

The villagers were fed up with Ram's fussing and worrying. But should Ram be killed to end their misery? The king's solution explains why we sometimes shudder on a stormy night.

How Lightning Came to Be

Inspired by a Nigerian tale

There was once a mother sheep whose son, Ram, loved her so much that he reacted to her every sound. If she sighed even softly, Ram became alarmed. If she gave a moan under her breath, he would **gnash** his teeth and toss his horns about. And if she groaned aloud, he became **distressed.**

This wouldn't have been so bad if Ram were an ordinary sheep. But he wasn't. His ironlike hooves created sparks whenever he walked on the rocky soil around his home. And when he was in distress over his mother, the sparks would fly! More than once, he had nearly burned their simple hut to the ground.

So it came to pass that whenever the villagers heard the voice of Mother Sheep, they would rush to fill buckets of water.

Once Mother Sheep forgot and "baa-ed" out loud from happiness. At once Ram rushed up and down among the homes in the village, spreading sparks left and right. His sparks set two fields of corn on fire. Another time he set two of the villagers' roofs aflame.

"My son," Mother Sheep would say. "Please don't alarm yourself over me. I'm just an old sheep. Nothing to get upset about."

"But, Mother, I can't help it," said the passionate young ram. "Anything that moves you in the least moves me even more."

One day Mother Sheep slipped and twisted her left front leg. Try as she might to **suppress** her pain, she couldn't help crying out sharply. An equally sharp cry rose up from the villagers. "Look out, here he comes! Water! Water!"

Ram went **berserk.** He galloped across fields and clearings. Sparks flew everywhere. Half the village burned to the ground.

The people angrily went to the king. "Do something before he fries us all," one old woman demanded. "We'd all be better off if Ram were killed," said another.

The king, however, was a kind-hearted fellow. He understood the son's **empathy** for his mother's feelings. He felt the same about his own beloved mother. When she became upset or moved by the slightest thing, he did too. Sometimes he became so **roused** by his mother's anger that he went to war.

So instead of having Ram killed, the king sent mother and son to live in the sky.

And they live there still. Sometimes you can hear Mother Sheep's voice in the thunder. And when lightning streaks across the sky, you can be sure that Ram is kicking up a fuss over his mother again.

INSIGHTS

This myth is from Nigeria, the homeland of the Yoruba people. Yoruba mythology tells of hundreds of gods—some major and others minor. Major gods, called the Orisha, rule huge regions such as the sky and earth. Minor gods rule over smaller areas such as villages.

What are the Orisha like? In many ways they resemble a family. Olorun is the father figure and rules over the sky. Olokun is the mother figure and rules over the earth.

The other gods act much like the children in a large family. They help each other, laugh at each other, and even plot against each other.

One of the most important Orisha is Shango, the god of thunder and lightning. Shango is an earth god. That is, he is a human being who became a god.

During his life, Shango was King of Oyo. At the end of his rule, Shango didn't die. Instead, he rose up to the sky along a golden chain and became the god of thunder and lightning. When the Yoruba hear thunder, they say *Kabiyesi!* This means, "Your Majesty, hail!"

Shango is also the god of fair play. He punishes those who lie, steal, and make evil magic. When he speaks, fire comes out of his mouth.

Shango's favorite wife is Oya, goddess of the River Niger. Oya is also known as the goddess of storms. When Shango rides the thunderstorms, Oya rides with him, blowing roofs off houses and uprooting trees.

WHY MOSSES AND VINES GROW ON TREES

VOCABULARY PREVIEW

Below is a list of words that appear in the story. Read the list and get to know the words before you read the story.

lush—thick; healthy
massing—gathering
mortally—resulting in death
petition—ask or request in a formal way
proposed—suggested
strikingly—uncommonly; unusually
valiantly—bravely

Main Characters

Amin—young man in love with Sayrah
Sayrah—beautiful young woman
Yengay—young man loved by Sayrah

*Why do mosses and vines
grow on trees? A romance
from the Bambara people of
western Africa gives one
answer to this question.*

Why Mosses and Vines Grow on Trees

Adapted from a Bambara tale

In a small village there lived a young Bambara man named Amin.[1] He deeply loved a young woman named Sayrah.[2]

However, Sayrah was devoted to a man named Yengay.[3] In fact, Sayrah and Yengay had been in love since they were very young. Everyone in the village knew about

---

[1] (a men´)
[2] (ser´ a)
[3] (yeng´ gā)

Sayrah and Yengay and expected them to marry.

But this didn't keep Amin from loving Sayrah. "My love is so great that I could even share her with Yengay," he declared. "But she must become my wife."

Amin asked his parents to **petition** Sayrah's father and mother for her hand. But they refused.

"Why must you be so blind?" asked Amin's mother. "This girl can feel nothing in her heart but love for Yengay. You would be unhappy with a woman like that for a wife."

Amin's parents tried to change his mind. First they brought him a young woman who was quite rich in farmland. Her fields were so grassy that cows left their pastures to graze in hers.

This young woman had admired Amin for some time. The whole village agreed that the young woman would make a good match for Amin.

But Amin said no. "I don't want land. I don't want cows. I want Sayrah."

His parents then brought him a young woman who was **strikingly** beautiful. When she walked, trees turned into firewood hoping to warm her feet. This young woman also had laid eyes on Amin—and she was interested. The villagers nodded their approval of this **proposed** match too.

Again Amin refused. "No woman is as beautiful in my eyes as Sayrah."

Well, this went on for some time. But Amin would have nothing to do with any women his parents found. Finally Amin's parents gave up. They talked with Sayrah's parents.

"Sayrah loves only Yengay," said the girl's parents. "But she may marry your son if she can bring Yengay to live with her. That is, if Yengay's parents approve of such an unusual arrangement."

And so it happened. Amin happily took Sayrah as his wife. But Sayrah brought Yengay with her.

Sayrah was obedient to Amin, but she remained faithful to Yengay. Before Sayrah served her new husband his dinner, she served Yengay. Before Amin's clothes could be washed, Sayrah washed Yengay's.

Amin soon realized that Sayrah loved Yengay more than she loved him. When he complained, she would gently remind him of their wedding agreement.

The village gossips took note of all of the goings-on in this strange household. "Amin is a fool," they said to each other. "Can't he see that Sayrah still loves Yengay?"

One day word came that the village was going to be attacked. In fact, the enemy was **massing** on the horizon. All unmarried men were to report to the king. Unmarried women would serve as cooks and nurses.

Since Yengay was still single, he immediately took up his spear and marched off to war.

With Yengay gone, Amin thought that he would have Sayrah to himself. But that night the enemy's armies began to march on the village. Things went badly for the village forces in the first attack. Everyone was asked to defend the village.

Sayrah immediately packed Amin's clothes. Then she packed hers. "I must go to Yengay," she told him. "He's on the front line."

"Can't we walk to the battle together?" Amin asked in despair.

"No. I want to walk alone," Sayrah said. "I'll meet you on the battlefield."

So Amin went alone with a heavy heart. When he arrived, he saw Yengay **valiantly** shooting arrow after arrow. Behind Yengay stood Sayrah.

Just then enemy arrows began to fall all around them. One hit Yengay and he fell to the ground. Another found its mark in Amin's chest. Sayrah screamed and rushed to the **mortally** wounded Amin.

"I love you, Amin," she whispered over and over. Her words reached the dying Amin's ears just in time. At last, in death, his love for Sayrah was returned. As Sayrah knelt beside him, another arrow found her heart.

It is said that where Sayrah died, a tree sprang up that gave no fruit. Where Yengay died, a strong, thick vine grew up the tree trunk. And where Amin died, **lush** green mosses spread across the ground. Eventually the moss covered both vine and tree.

You may not believe this. But the Old Ones say that this is why mosses and vines grow on trees.

INSIGHTS

This myth is from the Bambara people. The Bambara homeland is in western Africa, in what was once called Mali. In the 13th century, Mali was a large trading empire. Its rulers were famous for being just and fair.

Trade caravans brought the Islamic religion to Mali in the 1100s. Eventually, many people in both northern and western Africa became followers of Islam.

The Bambara are famous for their masks. Masks are used all over Africa in dances and religious rituals. But the Bambara have one mask that is found nowhere else.

This mask has two antelopes—a small one perched on top of a larger one. This unique headdress represents the *chi wara*—an important figure in Bambara tradition. The chi wara is a spirit who took the form of an antelope and taught the people to farm. Dancers wear these masks when they pray for a good harvest.

WHY THE BAT SLEEPS UPSIDE DOWN

VOCABULARY PREVIEW

Below is a list of words that appear in the story. Read the list and get to know the words before you read the story.

circumstances—conditions; events
dense—heavy; thick
dismay—fright; fear
ignorance—lack of knowledge; inexperience
laconic—brief; short
smirked—grinned; gave a stuck-up smile
stammered—stuttered

Main Characters

Bat—messenger for the High God
Chameleon—another messenger for the High God
High God—Supreme God
Monkey—another messenger for the High God

The poor bat was a nervous and uneasy creature. One time he became so embarrassed that he forgot the High God's orders. To this day, Bat is still trying to make up for his mistake.

Why the Bat Sleeps Upside Down

Inspired by a tale from the Kono people of Sierra Leone

In the beginning of time, Bat slept right side up. He leaned upright with his head tucked under his right wing, as chickens do.

Now Bat was a nervous sort. That's why he flipped and flapped and jerked when he flew.

One day a messenger from the High God appeared at Bat's door. The High God had an important task for the nervous animal. Bat was to present himself at the palace the next morning at eight o'clock sharp.

This was quite an honor for Bat. Usually the High God called upon Chameleon or Spider or Monkey to do his important work. But Bat was so nervous about serving the High God that he didn't sleep at all that night. And though Bat left for the palace two hours early, his wings trembled so much that he was half an hour late. Of course, being late made Bat even more nervous.

Finally God called Bat into His presence. "I have an important mission for you," God said in a stern voice. "This basket must be taken to the moon immediately."

God continued His orders as He slipped a little basket made of black and purple grasses around Bat's neck. "Go directly to the moon. Talk to no one. And under no **circumstances** should you look inside the basket."

With eager wings, the little Bat started on his mission.

Not far along, he saw Chameleon. Forgetting God's order, Bat called, "I'm a carrier for the High God."

Chameleon rolled one eye slowly up toward Bat. "What do you carry?" he asked in his **laconic** manner.

"This basket, for the moon." Bat lifted his chin proudly.

"What's in the basket?" Chameleon asked.

"Why, I don't know," Bat **stammered.** "God didn't say."

Chameleon dismissed Bat with an "umh humph" and slowly crawled on.

Bat sped on and soon flew over Monkey swinging in a tree.

"I'm a carrier for the High God," he sang.

"Congratulations," said Monkey. "And what do you carry?"

"This basket for the moon," Bat said.

The monkey asked him what was in the basket. When the Bat said he didn't know, Monkey **smirked.** "Some of us *carry* things and some of us just *haul* them."

Bat felt even more embarrassed at his **ignorance.** He flew down to the ground to a small clearing. Carefully he removed the basket from around his neck and set it on the ground. Slowly he pulled back the lid for a quick look.

Instantly a **dense,** dark shape swept out of the basket and flew up toward the moon. It covered everything with a deep velvet darkness.

With a cry of **dismay,** Bat darted after the darkness. But it was too late. Bat flew about for hours, trying to capture the darkness and return it to the basket.

But in time, the sun rose. Suddenly the darkness disappeared.

In fear of God's anger, Bat rushed home to his cave. Trying to hide from God, he hung himself upside down in a corner. He tucked both wings over his body and head and cried himself to sleep.

When Bat finally awoke, he saw that darkness had returned. Bat shot out into the dark night. He tried and tried to catch darkness to put it back in the basket.

"Please, darkness, return to this basket," he cried. "I must take you to the moon where you belong."

Of course, the darkness didn't reply. Nor did it climb into the basket.

To this day Bat chases darkness and sleeps upside down in caves. This is also how night came to be let loose into the world.

INSIGHTS

This story is from the Kono people of Sierra Leone in western Africa. Traditional Kono communities have an interesting educational practice. When young people reach the age of fifteen, they are initiated into secret societies—one for men and one for women.

The boys' initiation lasts from November to May. During this time, the boys stay in a special camp. They sleep on the ground and avoid people from the village. Older men teach the boys how to be adults. When the boys return to the village, they are considered men and they become members of the male secret society.

The Kono women have a similar but separate secret society with its own rituals.

Another explanation of why the bat hangs upside down in caves is told in a myth from the Congo. In this myth, the bat was a wealthy king. One day King Lightning paid Bat a visit. During the visit, Lightning spied a beautiful platter that belonged to Bat. Lightning asked King Bat if he could have the platter. But Bat refused, saying the platter was a symbol of his kingship.

Lightning became furious. He stormed back to the sky and destroyed all of King Bat's buildings and cattle. Because of Lightning's actions, King Bat vowed never to look toward the sky again. Instead, he hangs upside down in caves.

RIGHT AND WRONG

The Snake and the Princess

The Moon Prince

Point of View

While myths can be entertaining and fun to read, they can also teach moral lessons. Very often, the lessons are simple and straightforward. In general, humble and kind characters are rewarded. Selfish and greedy characters suffer in the end.

But sometimes a myth might present a character with a difficult life choice. For example, how should a prince handle his anger when an injustice is done to him? Or how should a young man act when asked to hide his true identity? The myths in this section deal with such difficult questions.

African storytellers often tell their listeners the moral or lesson of a story. But sometimes the tellers invite the audience to give their opinions. They might even stop the action of the story to ask the listeners what they think a character should do next.

Now it's your turn. What do you think?

THE SNAKE AND THE PRINCESS

VOCABULARY PREVIEW

Below is a list of words that appear in the story. Read the list and get to know the words before you read the story.

conniving—scheming; sneaky
controversy—argument
ebony—black
inherit—receive property from a relative
modesty—humbleness; self-control
pillaging—robbing; looting
spiteful—hateful; cruel
sullenly—gloomily
venom—poison

Main Characters

Ntombinde—princess
Queen Manyoka—mother of Snake Prince
Snake Prince—oldest son of Queen Manyoka

Donald E. Pierre

*He was a snake with the heart of a man. She was a princess
with the heart of a warrior. Only her courage could save
them both.*

The **Snake**
and the
Princess

Adapted from a tale from the Congo

In some ways, Ntombinde[1] was an ordinary princess.
She behaved just as you would expect a princess to
behave. She was compassionate and caring. And she
always thought of others before herself.

But in other ways, Ntombinde was a very extraordinary princess. For example, she was very curious.
She often went exploring by herself, just to see how
other people lived.

[1] (tum bin´ dā)

But most of all, Ntombinde was very courageous. Once she fought off a band of thieves who were **pillaging** the countryside. Another time she challenged a river monster to a fight and triumphed.

Now the king was proud of his daughter. Yet he was embarrassed by her as well.

One day the king spoke to his wife about Ntombinde. "Where's her **modesty?**" he asked. "How will we ever find someone to marry her? She's just too outspoken. She must get that from you."

"I think that whoever becomes Ntombinde's lover will be a lucky man," the queen said with a playful smile. "For a *real* man, our daughter's courage and outspokenness will not be a threat. Who knows, Ntombinde may even save a man's life."

That spring Ntombinde was invited to a wedding many kingdoms away. As always, she traveled alone.

But along the way, night fell with Ntombinde far from her destination. As luck would have it, she came upon a small kingdom. She learned that it was ruled by Queen Manyoka[2]— widow of the late king. Ntombinde asked the queen for lodging at the royal palace.

Queen Manyoka graciously took her in and led her to a beautifully decorated room.

"Before I leave you, I must tell you the story of this room," the queen said. "Then you can decide if you wish to stay in it."

"I'm ready to listen," replied Ntombinde with enthusiasm. This sounded like an adventure and, as you know, Ntombinde loved adventure!

"Long ago, the king and I lived in happiness with our family," began the queen. "We had four children. Besides our eldest son, we had two younger sons and a daughter.

"Then **controversy** set in," continued the queen sadly. "The younger children thought it unfair that their oldest brother was to **inherit** the throne.

"Now our younger children were **spiteful** and lazy. On the

[2] (man yō´ ka)

other hand, our elder son was hardworking, intelligent, and caring. Little wonder he became our favorite child.

"We tried to keep the younger children happy. We even increased their inheritance. But as time went on, the three youngest became more and more jealous.

"Finally they paid an evil sorcerer[3] to get rid of their innocent brother. The sorcerer cast a spell that changed our beloved son into a snake."

The queen paused. With difficulty she finished her story. "The jealous action of our youngest children broke the king's heart. Finally he died of grief.

"The sad thing is, the young ones regretted their action. They were horrified by the sorcerer's power. Unfortunately they could do nothing to break the spell.

"We have since found out that only a maiden pure in heart can change my son back into a man."

"Have many women tried to save your son?" asked Ntombinde.

"Many have tried," Queen Manyoka replied. "But they only wanted our son's riches. He sensed their greed, and his snake heart hardened. He killed them all."

Queen Manyoka looked into Ntombinde's eyes. "Now do you still want to spend the night here?" she asked quietly.

"Yes," was Ntombinde's immediate reply. "I am curious to meet your son."

With that, the queen ordered a huge meal of meat and palm juice put on the table. Then she opened a window in the room. "Each night he returns to eat," she explained. "Perhaps you will be the one to bring a change of heart in my Snake Prince. Nothing else—not even the gods—can do it."

With these words, the queen turned and left the room.

Now common sense warned Ntombinde not to sleep near an open window. And she certainly didn't want to be surprised by a large snake. So she vowed to stay awake all night.

When daylight came, Ntombinde was still awake. The food was still there. But outside the window she found a patch

---

[3] A sorcerer is a magician.

of gold and black snakeskin.

"My son has been here," Manyoka said when she saw the skin. "And he didn't bother you. That's a good sign. Will you stay another night?"

The courageous Ntombinde agreed. Again Manyoka set out food and again Ntombinde stayed awake. In the morning the food remained uneaten. But this time servants found two patches of snakeskin outside.

"I think he's studying you," said Manyoka.

"I'm studying him too," said Ntombinde.

Manyoka asked Ntombinde to stay one more night. And now the younger sons and daughter begged her to stay too.

"You who made him suffer so now wish for his return?" Ntombinde asked with surprise. "Do you plan to give him yet more pain?"

"Oh no. All of this is our fault," admitted one brother.

"It was all so long ago," added the daughter. "We were selfish fools. Our tutors said we had the hardest heads in the whole kingdom."

"We were too busy listening to the gods of greed to learn anything," said the other brother. "And too lazy. We raced horses all day and danced all night. Now your courage is our only hope of bringing our brother back."

On this third night Ntombinde pretended to be asleep. Finally around midnight she heard a noise outside. Through half-closed eyes she saw a huge serpent glide in through the window. The Snake Prince coiled his golden-black body and lifted his head. Then he stared into Ntombinde's face.

The snake's face was that of a handsome man. Ntombinde had never seen such a sad face. Her heart melted as she fell in love with the Snake Prince.

But then the snake spoke. His face twisted into a mask of evil. "Why are you here?" he hissed harshly.

"Because you've already suffered more than most men ever will," Ntombinde replied. "And because your sadness touches my heart."

"You lie!" spat the snake. "You're just like all the rest. You hope to become my bride. And you want to be queen of this land so that you can get your hands on my riches."

"I don't need your riches," Ntombinde replied with fire in her eyes. "I'm already rich. I'm compassionate, curious, and courageous. And I'm not afraid to speak my mind."

"You lie. You're **conniving** and greedy." The snake towered over her. "I hate my brothers and sister for what they did to me. I hate everyone. First I'll kill you with my **venom.** Then I'll devour you."

The snake opened his mouth, showing his huge fangs. But Ntombinde stood her ground.

"Stop that!" Ntombinde said sternly. "In your heart you're still a man. But your heart has been poisoned by the hate of a snake. The ways of a snake cannot live in the heart of a man."

The snake was surprised by the young woman's outburst. He closed his mouth and stared at her in wonder.

But Ntombinde had just begun. "Devour me?" she laughed. "You do, and I'll give you a stomachache you won't forget. And if you call me a liar again, I'll stomp on your tail."

The Snake Prince pulled in his tail and backed away. "You're not big enough for a meal anyway," the snake said **sullenly.**

Still watching her, the snake slithered to the table and began to eat. Ntombinde thought she saw a smile dance briefly around the serpent's mouth.

Slowly Ntombinde approached the table. As if in a trance, the Snake Prince froze. Then without warning, the young princess gently kissed the prince on his snakeskin cheek.

The Snake Prince let out a deep sigh. The prince's human spirit broke through the snake's hateful hold on his heart. The snakeskin fell away.

Before Ntombinde stood a tall, handsome, **ebony**-skinned man wrapped in golden robes. The grateful prince immediately asked Ntombinde to marry him.

Ntombinde just smiled. "Let me see what my father has to say first."

INSIGHTS

The Snake and the Princess" comes from the Congo in central Africa. This part of Africa was isolated from the rest of the world for thousands of years. For this reason, the people of the Congo were unknown to the outside world until the 19th century.

The snake appears often in myths from the Congo. For example, the snake plays an important role in several creation stories from the region.

In one story, God called the first man and the snake together. Then he placed two baskets before them. Without saying what was in the baskets, God invited the man to choose one. The unlucky man chose the basket that contained death.

The snake was more fortunate. He got the basket that contained the secret of shedding his skin. By casting off his old skin for a new one, the snake learned how to live forever.

It's no wonder that snakes play important roles in myths from the Congo. A look at just one of the snakes of the region might explain why.

The African rock python is indeed impressive. This snake can grow up to 30 feet long and can reach a weight of 300 pounds. And this snake can be very dangerous—it has been known to swallow humans.

Despite this threat, many central Africans believe pythons help their crops grow. For this reason, farmers leave part of their fields unplowed. The farmers hope that a python will live in the unused area and make their land more fertile.

Snakes are important in other parts of Africa as well. According to the mythology of the Fon people of western Africa, a giant snake helped form the earth. Indeed, the snake still holds the world together. The serpent coils 3,500 times above the earth and 3,500 times below it. One Fon tradition says that if the snake ever moves, the world will fall apart.

THE MOON PRINCE

VOCABULARY PREVIEW

Below is a list of words that appear in the story. Read the list
and get to know the words before you read the story.

apprentice—student; beginner
banished—sent away as punishment
coveted—much wanted; desired
decreed—ordered; commanded
flamboyant—showy; stylish
hearth—fireplace
heir—one who will become the next ruler
mockery—a joke

Main Characters

Ironsmith—foster father to Moon Prince
King Khoedi-Sefubeng—father of Moon Prince
Latifa—second favorite wife of the king
Moon Prince—son of the king and Morongoe
Morongoe—favorite wife of the king; mother of Moon Prince
Mouse—friend of Morongoe

Sometimes even small, humble creatures can make a big difference. In this story, you'll learn how Mouse helped the Moon Prince regain his rightful place.

THE MOON PRINCE

Inspired from a tale of the Sotho people

Mouse is the most humble of all creatures. She doesn't wear **flamboyant** feathers or flowing fur. Her voice is not pleasing to hear, and she cannot fly. Dressed simply in earth tones, Mouse industriously gathers seeds and straw for **hearth** and home.

Quiet and rarely seen, Mouse works hard and long during day and darkness. But not only for herself. She'll help anyone who needs her. They say she even helped the Moon Prince regain his rightful throne. This is how it happened.

Mouse lived in a cottage on the royal palace grounds of King Khoedi-Sefubeng.[1] This cottage was the quarters of Queen Morongoe.[2] Of the King's ten wives, Morongoe was his favorite.

King Sefubeng was so beloved that people said he was descended from the gods. As proof, they pointed to the birth-mark on his chest. This birthmark was shaped like the moon and gave forth a beautiful golden light.

Each time a wife of the king became heavy with child, there was great rejoicing. Mouse rejoiced too. She loved motherhood. She was especially glad when Morongoe became pregnant. She loved Morongoe, who left crumbs in secret corners just for her.

Even though Morongoe was the King's favorite wife, it was not certain that her child would take over the throne. The king **decreed** that only the baby born with the moon-shaped birthmark would be his **heir.**

As it happened, the other wives gave birth before Morongoe—and all had sons. But not one of the sons had a birthmark.

Then came Morongoe's turn to give birth. Latifa,[3] the king's second favorite wife, came to help. To Morongoe's surprise, her son was born with the **coveted** birthmark.

But Latifa showed no happiness. She was jealous by nature. And when she saw the birthmark on the child's chest, she quickly left the cottage.

That evening, Mouse sat on the bed admiring the baby while Morongoe slept. A beautiful golden light filled the room. The light shone from the baby's chest as if a full moon were rising there.

Suddenly someone entered the room. Mouse saw that it was Latifa's nursemaid.[4] Silently the nursemaid slipped in and took Morongoe's baby. In the baby's place the nursemaid left a monkey.

Mouse followed the woman into the night. As she trailed

---

[1] (ku hu´ dē se fu´ bing) Khoedi-Sefubeng means "moon-in-chest."
[2] (mōr ong´ gō ē)
[3] (la tē´ fa)
[4] A nursemaid is a person who helps take care of a newborn baby.

the nursemaid, Mouse called friends to help her. They saw the woman enter a stable.

The animals peeked into the stable as the woman put the baby on the floor. "Wait right here, little one," she said. "I'll be right back. I just need to find a knife."

Was she going to kill the child? Quickly Mouse and her friends picked up the baby and carried it away.

"What should we do with the Moon Prince?" one mouse asked.

"We must keep him hidden," replied another.

"Take him to the cow pasture," ordered Mouse. "Surely there is a cow that can feed him milk until we can return the baby to Morongoe."

Mouse returned to Morongoe's cottage at dawn, just as the king arrived. He had come to see the infant. Of course, he wanted to know if his youngest son carried the birthmark.

But behind the king came Latifa. And before Morongoe could share the good news, Latifa lifted the wraps from around the monkey.

"Morongoe makes a **mockery** of your throne," Latifa shouted. "Look! She didn't even give birth to a human child."

Bewildered and embarrassed, the King **banished** Morongoe from his grounds. "And take this ugly monkey with you!" he ordered.

Latifa saw to it that the whole kingdom heard about Morongoe's "monkey" child. And shortly thereafter, the son of Latifa was named heir to the throne. As for Latifa—she became Queen Latifa.

Poor Morongoe was forced to leave the kingdom altogether. She left not knowing if her son was alive or dead. But in her son's place, she carried the monkey on her shoulder. No one knew where she went.

Meanwhile, Mouse spent the next several months watching over the Moon Prince. She had found a stable where he could be kept warm and dry. The cows gave him milk to drink.

But one evening Latifa happened to pass by. When she saw moonlight coming from inside the stable, she immediately knew who was inside.

"I thought you were dead!" Latifa hissed. "Well, you soon will be!"

Ever watchful, Mouse heard Latifa. And as Latifa reached to pick up the child, Mouse ran across the woman's feet. Latifa shrieked and fled.

Mouse knew that Latifa would be back. So she led the boy to a haystack. Then Mouse sent out word that she needed help.

A relative who lived in the marketplace returned with good news. "An ironsmith[5] there seeks a young **apprentice,**" the messenger said. "Perhaps he'll take the boy in."

Away they went through the night. The ironsmith was surprised to see a boy at his door. But when he saw the birthmark, he knew the child's true identity. "Come in," he said. "You'll be safe with me."

And so he was. Years passed and the boy grew into a handsome young man. The boy loved the ironsmith and learned much from him. But he felt incomplete, as if he were missing something.

Then one day the ironsmith took the young man aside. "You probably know by now that I'm not your father," the ironsmith began. "I can tell you who I think your father is."

Then the ironsmith told the prince about the king's birthmark and his mother's banishment. He also told him of Queen Latifa. "I have never trusted her," the ironsmith said. "Her son became heir to the throne too soon after your mother's banishment."

From that day on, the prince longed for the day when he could let the world know who he really was. He wanted to meet King Sefubeng and reveal the birthmark on his chest. As it was, the prince had to keep his birthmark hidden for fear that Latifa might learn of his whereabouts.

One day Mouse heard that King Sefubeng was to visit the ironsmith. It seemed that the king needed a special set of knives that only the ironsmith could produce. The ironsmith was flattered by the royal visit. But he was concerned about

---

[5] An ironsmith is a person who makes useful objects out of iron.

the prince as well.

"Stay hidden in the closet," he told the boy. "Latifa wouldn't be pleased to hear that you're still alive. Keep your robe on to hide your moonlight. It's best this way."

The prince agreed, but he hated having to hide. "I'm a man," he told himself aloud. "Men don't hide. Men defend what is theirs."

On the morning of the king's visit, the marketplace was especially busy. Vendors set out their best goods in their stalls. Others fought for spots along the king's route. One woman in a headwrap and shawl sat near the ironsmith's door. Despite the orders of the king's men, she wouldn't leave.

"Let her alone," the ironsmith said. "She hasn't done anything wrong."

Mouse sat with the prince in the closet. They watched the festivities through a large crack in the closet door. Soon they heard drums and shouts. The king was coming.

Mouse saw that Queen Latifa sat outside in her royal carriage. When King Sefubeng entered the shop, the ironsmith fell to his knees in honor of the king. Then the king and the ironsmith got down to business.

When they were finished, the king turned to go. Out of the corner of his eye, he saw golden light shining through the crack in the closet. "What light shines from inside that closet?" he asked. "It looks like moonlight."

Upon hearing the king's question, the prince pushed open the door. Then with a majestic motion, he pulled his robe away from his chest. "I'm the true heir to the throne," the Moon Prince shouted. "I carry your birthmark. I'm your son, and my mother is Morongoe."

At that moment, the woman in the headwrap burst through the door. Of course, it was Morongoe.

When she saw her son, she cried aloud. "I always believed you were alive, and here you are!" Then she turned to the astonished king. "At last I can tell you my side of the story."

When she finished, the king had Latifa imprisoned. He welcomed the Moon Prince and Morongoe back into the palace.

The Moon Prince accepted the invitation to live with his father. But Morongoe declined. She said she was happier being with humble, common people. That is where she stayed. And Mouse and the monkey stayed with her.

INSIGHTS

The homeland of the Sotho people is in southern Africa. The Sotho are the descendants of one of the Bantu groups who migrated from the Congo region nearly 2,000 years ago.

The Sotho tell many epic tales about heroes like the Moon Prince. As in this story, something unusual happened at the hero's birth. Because of his unusual birth, people knew he was special. But the hero had to face many dangers before he became king.

These epics traveled with the Sotho when they left the Congo. People called "rememberers" memorized the long stories so they would not be forgotten during the journey to the south.

Like many Bantu groups, the traditional Sotho measure a family's wealth by the amount of cattle it owns. A man usually gives his bride's family at least 15 head of cattle. Men raise the cattle and clear land for crops while women do the farming.

POINT OF VIEW

VOCABULARY PREVIEW

Below is a list of words that appear in the story. Read the list and get to know the words before you read the story.

bellowing—roaring
perspective—point of view; way of seeing
structure—shape; design

Main Characters

First man
Second man

This story ends with a question. Which of the two men was right? It's all in how you look at things.

oint of View

It has been said that a mountain to an ant is but a pebble to a giraffe. In other words, how things appear depends upon your **perspective.**

This is as true with people as it is with animals.

There once were two men going to market when it became dark.

"Day is ending, for the sun sets," said one.

"Oh no," said the other. "Night begins, for the moon rises."

The two men began to argue. Which man was right?

Still arguing, the men searched for lodging.

Soon they found a room for the night and prepared for bed.

One man said, "We must sleep at the foot of the bed. That way we'll face east when morning comes."

"Then that part of the bed becomes the head," said the other.

"You're stupid," cried the first man, pointing to one end of the bed. "Look at the **structure** of the bed. See the head of the bed?" He pointed to another end. "See the foot of the bed?"

"There is no head, nor is there a foot," said the other. "A head has eyes and a nose and a mouth. A foot has a heel and toes. A bed has none of these things."

So the men argued back and forth. Which man was right?

(If you must know, they both ended up sleeping on the floor.)

In the middle of the night, one man began to snore. The other man began to walk in his sleep. The sleepwalker dreamed he was off on a great mission. Then he tripped over his companion.

The snorer dreamed he was being chased by a **bellowing** elephant. He let out a loud snore. Both men awoke at the same time.

The snorer looked at the sleepwalker standing over him. The sleepwalker looked at the snorer with his mouth still open.

"You woke me up with your sleepwalking," the snorer said.

"No, you woke me up with your snoring," the sleepwalker said.

They fussed until daylight came.

Then one man said night was gone because the sun was up. The other man said day was here because the moon had set.

And so they fussed some more.

Which man was right?

Does it matter?

INSIGHTS

Dilemma stories such as "Point of View" are told all over Africa. Here is another example from Togo in western Africa.

A man sent his three sons on a journey. After a year, each son had found one gift for his father. Before returning home, the sons met to share their findings.

The youngest son had a mirror that let the viewer see all over the country. The second son had sandals that took the wearer anyplace in the country with just one step. The eldest carried a gourd full of medicine.

The sons looked in the magic mirror to see how their father was doing. They saw that he was dead and already buried. They used the magic sandals to rush to the father's grave. Then the eldest poured his medicine onto the grave. The result? Their father came back to life.

Now which of the sons' gifts helped the father the most?